7

SATOSHI
WAGAHARA

ILLUSTRATION BY
029 (ONIKU)

THE DEVIL IS A PART-TIMER!

CONTENTS!

THE DEVIL IS A PART-TIMER

SATOSHI WAGAHARA

ILLUSTRATED BY 029 (ONIKU)

7

YEN
ON
NEW YORK

THE DEVIL IS A PART-TIMER!, Volume 7
SATOSHI WAGAHARA, ILLUSTRATION BY 029 (ONIKU)

Translation by Kevin Gifford
Cover art by 029 (oniku)

HATARAKU MAOUSAMA!, Volume 7
© SATOSHI WAGAHARA 2013
All rights reserved.
Edited by ASCII MEDIA WORKS
First published in 2013 by KADOKAWA CORPORATION, Tokyo.

English translation rights arranged with KADOKAWA CORPORATION,
Tokyo, through Tuttle-Mori Agency, Inc., Tokyo.

Yen On
1290 Avenue of the Americas
New York, NY 10104

Visit us at yenpress.com
facebook.com/yenpress
twitter.com/yenpress
yenpress.tumblr.com
instagram.com/yenpress

First Yen On Edition: April 2017

Yen On is an imprint of Yen Press, LLC.
The Yen On name and logo are trademarks of Yen Press,
LLC.

The publisher is not responsible for websites (or their
content) that are not owned by the publisher.

Library of Congress Cataloging-in-Publication Data
Names: Wagahara, Satoshi. | 029 (Light novel
illustrator) illustrator. | Gifford, Kevin, translator.
Title: The devil is a part-timer! / Satoshi Wagahara ;
illustration by 029 (oniku) ; translation by Kevin
Gifford.
Other titles: Hataraku Maousama! English
Description: First Yen On edition. | New York, NY :
Yen On, 2015–
Identifiers: LCCN 2015028390|
ISBN 9780316383127 (v. 1 : pbk.) |
ISBN 9780316385015 (v. 2 : pbk.) |
ISBN 9780316385022 (v. 3 : pbk.) |
ISBN 9780316385039 (v. 4 : pbk.) |
ISBN 9780316385046 (v. 5 : pbk.) |
ISBN 9780316385060 (v. 6 : pbk.) |
ISBN 9780316469364 (v. 7 : pbk.)
Subjects: | CYAC: Fantasy.
Classification: LCC PZ7.1.W34 Ha 2015 | DDC
[Fic]—dc23
LC record available at
http://lccn.loc.gov/2015028390

ISBNs: 978-0-316-46936-4 (paperback)
978-0-316-47262-3 (ebook)

1 3 5 7 9 10 8 6 4 2

LSC-C

Printed in the United States of America

THE DEVIL PLEDGES TO STAY LEGITIMATE

Perhaps it could be called the ultimate move of self-sacrifice, the equivalent of cutting his own throat in order to save the team. He was defeated in battle, unable to turn the tides of war; he was surrounded, with only a meager crew of fellow warriors. His master's life was gradually being chipped away, too, under the unwitting spell of one of his own corrupted generals.

He knew the time had come to make a decision. To turn the tables on this desperate scene, he knew he had to take action on his own. He bowed his head to his master as the man dined even now on the tainted food the enemy had provided.

"...My liege."

"Mm? What, Ashiya?"

Sadao Maou turned to him, his eyes clouded and bleary. His master had been tortured by his foes, beaten down until he was at the bottommost dregs of his energy and motivation. He was being fed far, far more than his stomach ever had a chance of storing. The pall of death was coming into focus on his face even now.

"I would most humbly ask you for some time off."

"...Huh?"

"Wha?"

"What?!"

"Uhh…"

"Yawwn…"

For the group piled into the narrow confines of Devil's Castle, aka Room 201 of the sixty-year-old Villa Rosa Sasazuka apartment building, each had their own reaction as they stared agape at the kneeling demon named Shirou Ashiya.

✳

"Wow," Emi Yusa—better known as the Hero Emilia and the Devil King's One True Enemy—said with a blank stare at Ashiya. "Can I take this as a sign that the Devil King's Army is collapsing?"

She had been in the process of taking up the collar of one Hanzou Urushihara—formerly known as the fallen angel Lucifer, and now more properly known as an unemployed freeloader—in order to toss him out the window. Her attention, diverted by Ashiya's sudden bombshell, made her grip loosen to the point that Urushihara fell limply to the tatami-mat floor instead.

"Yowch…," he murmured as he passed out, a hairbreadth away from asphyxiation.

By mere seconds he had avoided his final punishment: His mortal enemy had discovered the tracking device he had snuck into her bag. In many ways, he should've been glad to survive with his life.

But it was Ashiya's master, Sadao Maou himself, who was the most thrown by his faithful assistant's request for leave.

"Time off? What do you mean…?"

Compared to the glory days, when he had led the combined forces of the demon realms to a breathtaking conquest of every inhabited corner of Ente Isla, even Maou had to admit that he hadn't done much devilish in nature lately. But was that really enough to make Shirou Ashiya, his Great Demon General Alciel and most trusted of confidants through decades of political intrigue and bloody battles, wish to part ways with him?

Maybe this was about him using all the demonic power he'd

gained in the battle against Sariel to repair the collateral damage done to Tokyo's infrastructure. But he thought that was water under the bridge by now; he'd spent a good hour pleading his case to Ashiya, convincing him that it was the best thing he could have done under the circumstances.

But it was Chiho Sasaki, the only normal human being currently in Devil's Castle, who spoke up nervously in response.

"Um… This isn't because I overstepped my boundaries or anything, is it?"

She was part of the crew at the MgRonald fast-food joint in front of Hatagaya rail station. She was also the only person in the world who knew the truth behind the Devil's Castle denizens and the world of Ente Isla itself—and despite that, she still took a liking to Maou, Devil King or not. She was here to provide him with a home-cooked meal, in fact—something she now did on regular occasions.

"I…I mean, if me and Suzuno cooking for you guys is taking work away from you, Ashiya, I could totally…"

"Er, no," Ashiya hurriedly replied. "It's nothing like that, Ms. Sasaki. In fact, getting to share in your kindness has been tremendously…helpful to me."

Ashiya's responsibilities in Devil's Castle mainly revolved around housework—cooking, laundry, cleaning, and balancing the checkbook. And, inevitably, when a househusband stays on the job for long enough, he can't help but grow bored of his own cooking. Along those lines, Chiho's cuisine was one of the few things spicing up his life at the moment.

"Then what kind of nonsense is this?" asked a dubious Suzuno Kamazuki—aka Crestia Bell, cleric of the Church that dominated politics in Ente Isla's Western Island, and now living in Room 202 down the hall—as she stacked up the empty plastic containers she had brought her food over in. "Both myself and Emilia would welcome the idea of the Devil King's Army falling apart and being scattered to the four winds, but doing so without any reason strikes me as…unusual."

Suzuno might have been providing food to her neighbors, but she was every bit the demons' enemy as Emi was. Thus, she fed them dishes made with Church-sanctified ingredients, just as harmful to them—perhaps even more so—as processed sugars and trans fats. It did wonders to keep the Devil's Castle budget in the black, but Ashiya always greeted the act with a resigned sneer.

Amid the silence, the Great Demon General took a quick look at Chiho, then Emi, before sadly shaking his head.

"…I apologize, my liege…"

"Whoa, are you serious…?"

Maou, slowly realizing that Ashiya was being deadly serious with him, rose to his feet. His stomach, distended by Suzuno and Chiho's dual-pronged gastronomical attack, grumbled at him for it as he walked up to the kneeling Ashiya and grabbed him by the shoulders.

"Wh-what aren't you happy about?! Is this about the hot dog I bought from the convenience store on the way home from work the other day?! Or the store receipt you asked me to hang on to that I lost? Oh, man, I *told* you I bought that two-ply toilet paper by accident!"

Emi, watching behind Maou, gave him a forlorn look. *That* was all the frantic Devil King could think of? "If that's enough to make your Great Demon General want to leave," she remarked, "you should've demoted him long ago."

"No, Your Demonic Highness. I have no complaint with you, nor my work environment."

"You don't?"

To Emi, the fact that his master was in a panic about a hot dog—and the fact that he was making his top general toil as a house-husband for the foreseeable future—seemed like ample cause for complaint.

"It is just that…I fear our demonic forces will face ruin before long if this continues. My retiring from the front lines may allow us the chance to avoid this…"

"What are you talking about?!" Maou's gaze drilled into Ashiya's head. "I don't get it, man!" The two of them, master and servant, gave each other deeply troubled looks before Ashiya bowed his head in defeat.

"…Allow me to explain outside, my liege."

As the two of them left, the remainder of the group—save the unconscious Urushihara—looked at one another, puzzled.

When they returned through the door a few moments later, however, Maou was suddenly far more composed.

"Yo, Emi. Chi, too."

"…What?"

"Y-yes?"

"Sorry, but do you guys mind heading home? I'll explain later, but…for now, we need to be alone."

There was no longer any of the carefree breeziness that generally defined Maou's expression. In fact, there seemed to be a twinge of sadness to it.

"Sure, sure, whatever," Emi snorted. "Let's go, Chiho."

"B-but, Yusa…"

"Chi," Maou offered to his confused comrade. The single syllable conveyed that there was nothing to worry about.

"A-all right, but..," Chiho couldn't resist asking the question anyway. "Ashiya…you won't leave for good, will you?"

"…Don't worry," Maou replied, Ashiya himself apparently not in the mood for speech.

"Are you sure?" Emi interrupted. "Because if you're forming a guerrilla commando unit or something, I'm gonna kill you."

"Will you just *go* already?!" Maou said as he pushed his nemesis along, though he gave a quick, reassuring nod to Chiho along the way.

Ashiya was waiting by the front door, still silent. He received a small bow from Chiho and no acknowledgement whatsoever from Emi as they walked by. He sighed deeply as he watched them go.

"…Well. Quite a strange turn of events, this," Suzuno commented. As a Villa Rosa Sasazuka resident, she was the only visitor left in the room, although recent developments made her presence seem supremely awkward. "Right, then," she added as she began to stand up—only to be stopped by Ashiya stepping back inside.

"Wait, Crestia Bell. You are to stay."

"...What?"

Turning back, she found Ashiya giving her a glare as hard as his words, and Maou matching it.

Suddenly, she found herself in a far less secure position than before. Instinctively, she readied her body and removed the hairpin from her head. There was a flash of light, and then the hairpin was a massive hammer, one that seemed impossible for the slight woman to wield.

The cross-shaped hairpin was the agent she used to summon her Light of Iron magic, and the resulting warhammer was powerful enough to smash the giant electrical transformers that powered Shinjuku station. It could have flattened three destitute, powerless ex-demons like gnats, but being surrounded like this still made her nervous.

"Enough of this act," she said, attempting to keep them from making the first move. "Even alone, I could easily destroy you all."

"Silence, Bell," Ashiya continued. "We are seeking your assistance. You have no right to refuse."

"Such nonsense! I have no right, you say? With your puny powers, how could you ever support such a demand?"

"It's nothing like that," Maou said, crossing his arms as he shot a glance at the still-unresponsive Urushihara. "You simply have no choice, is all. The forty thousand yen Urushihara sucked out of our bank account for the tracking device... You're kind of at fault for that, too."

A garbage collection truck passed by the apartment building, offering garbled advertising guidance through a tinny speaker on its side.

"...Forty thousand?" Suzuno said, body still steeled for battle.

"Yeah. That's how much he spent on that gadget we used to find Chi and Emi after you and Sariel kidnapped them."

"That…gadget?"

Suzuno shot a surprised look at Urushihara. She had been wondering about that. How *did* Maou find her, doing Sariel's bidding on the tippy-top of the towering Tokyo Metropolitan Government Building?

"Is…is that even possible?"

"At any rate, you understand now, do you not?" Ashiya interjected. "Why you cannot turn down our behest, Bell?"

"Starting tomorrow, Ashiya's gonna go out and earn some money, so we can make up the forty thousand yen we spent on that thing for Chi's sake. That's why he asked me for a break. Even if I took on extra shifts at work, forty thousand's just an astronomical number. I could never make that up by myself."

"…Ugh."

Suzuno winced.

"I won't ask for half, but you're, like, at least a third responsible for this, right? Especially given how *you're* the one who kidnapped Chi."

"That…I…"

Suzuno attempted to counter, but found her spirit flagging. Her hammer fell helplessly to the tatami mats.

Several days before, Sariel descended from Ente Isla's version of heaven in search of the Better Half, the holy sword Emi housed within her body. The ensuing conflict almost resulted in a one-way ticket to another planet for Chiho. And Suzuno, in no position to defy the orders of an archangel, was the one who had lured Chiho to him.

In the end, the day had been saved by Maou's storming up the skyscraper and rescuing the trapped Emi and Chiho, neatly relieving Suzuno of her Ente Islan obligations along the way. The only reason he knew where to find them was because he followed the tracking device Urushihara had hidden inside Emi's bag.

"I can't really fault Urushihara for wasting our money this time, either. I mean, really, if it wasn't for that transmitter thingy, we'd have no idea what to do, and Chi and Emi would've been taken away from Earth long ago."

"Very much so, my liege…although I still question the need to spend forty thousand all at once."

"Well, hindsight is twenty-twenty and all that, isn't it, Ashiya? I know we need to teach Urushihara a lesson about his spending habits, but for *this* time, at least…"

Maou's eyes were on a now thoroughly despondent Suzuno.

"And that is why you sent Emilia and Chiho away, then?"

"Indeed," Ashiya nodded. "If we told Ms. Sasaki about this, you know how she would react. She would blame herself and offer to pay the entire sum. And we could not possibly accept any aid from Emilia. We used that device to rescue Ms. Sasaki, after all, *not* the likes of her. But there will be no palming responsibility for this off on Ms. Sasaki. We are the ones who got her involved with events on Ente Isla, after all."

A few moments ago, when Chiho spotted "Card payment: 40,000 yen; User: Dumbassyhara" in the Devil's Castle financial notebook, Ashiya made sure the subject remained firmly focused on Urushihara's extravagant shopping sprees mainly so Chiho wouldn't pick up on the truth and feel all guilty about it. It made things smoother all around if she and Emi just assumed Urushihara blew the money on the tracking device for no particular reason—none beyond the voyeuristic opportunities it allowed him. As a result, all Chiho was aware of was Urushihara's blatant invasion of Emi's privacy—something Emi subsequently half-murdered him for.

"…You are being remarkably thoughtful for a pack of horrid demons," Suzuno bitterly whispered. "So, what of it? What do you want from me? You wish me to repay some percentage of the cost?"

It seemed like a reasonable offer. Maou and Ashiya greeted it with abject scorn.

"Hah. You belittle us. We are the proud Devil King's Army! We would never accept the filthy lucre of the church we are destined to destroy!"

"Ashiya, you're talking crazy again."

"I am more than capable of making up for Urushihara's foolishness!

But to achieve that, I will have to leave Devil's Castle for a few days. Crestia Bell! While I am gone, you will cover the entire food bill of this domain!"

"Huh? Why?!"

It was not Suzuno, but Maou, whose voice rose up in protest.

"What is it, my liege?" Ashiya replied coolly.

"No, uh… I mean, why make Suzuno cook for us? Couldn't you just, like, make a few days' worth and leave us with that?"

"Whatever are you talking about? Ignoring the holy sanctification she places upon it, Suzuno's cuisine is both nutritious and delicious by homemade standards. It would save us a fortune in food bills."

"Oh, um…I am hardly *that* exceptional at it…"

"Don't compliment her, man! And *you* –don't *accept* the compliment, either! Besides, that makes us sound like a bunch of hoboes. Why can't we just take her money and—"

"*And*," Ashiya continued, "as long as Bell is cooking for you, there is no need for Chiho to suspect anything is amiss when she inevitably comes in to check on you. Two birds with one stone!"

Shrewd, Maou thought. The relationship between Chiho and Suzuno, if not outright hostile, certainly had a competitive aspect to it. Taking advantage of those feelings, while a little too calculating for Maou's tastes, seemed like a valid approach.

"Huh," he remarked. "You think?"

"Besides, Your Demonic Highness…without regular meals provided to the both of you, you will inevitably succumb to the temptations of outside junk food and waste even more of our money, will you not?"

"…Um."

Maou, who had just inadvertently confessed to exactly that, fell silent.

"Urushihara, for his part, would no doubt use my absence to gorge himself on pizza delivery and other trash. Health and nutrition are second-class concerns to him. If I had to pick between frozen franchise food packed with preservatives and MSG or freshly prepared meals with just a tad of sanctification added to it, I think the choice is blindingly obvious!"

"It is summer, though," Suzuno said, scratching one of her cheeks. "I'm afraid I have few raw ingredients left to work with."

"Regardless!" Ashiya declared, again ignoring all asides. "I will not be gone for long! For just a few days, as long as Ms. Sasaki and Emilia don't pick up on anything, you and Urushihara can keep things on the cheap. Soon, our ledger will return to the black and our Devil King's Army will be rescued from ruin! I tell you, it will work out!"

"Great," Suzuno and Maou agreed in tandem. Suzuno paused for a moment, nonplussed, then added:

"...All right, all right! You want my aid? You can have it! I felt just as poorly for Chiho as you did!"

"You are sounding awfully haughty, Crestia Bell..."

"...Ugh," Suzuno said, blushing in the face of the much taller demon. "I will help you. Is that what you want to hear?"

"...You're so loud, dudes. What's up?" Urushihara, choosing this exact moment to shift from unconsciousness to mere sleeping, sat up and rubbed his eyes.

"Urushihara, listen," Maou murmured.

"Huh?"

"Just watch your food, your cash, and your attitude, okay?"

"...Where'd that come from?"

Nobody answered the question.

✳

The following morning:

"The spices are over there, got it? We don't have very much rice left, but what we have is stored under the sink, inside that cabinet. Make sure you wash and dry the rice bin before pouring in more rice."

"...Right."

"The knives should be sharpened well enough, but the stone's also under the sink, should you need it. If you use any of our washcloths, wash them and hang them on this mini rack up here to dry."

"Very well…"

"And I must remind you, always make sure you thoroughly wash the rice cooker after each use. Lid and container, all right? Urushihara always leaves dried rice bits inside whenever he uses it. I'm talking both sides of the lid, too, do you understand?"

"All right! Just leave already!!"

Being lectured on kitchen etiquette was not Suzuno's idea of an enjoyable start to the day. She was hardly a slob herself, although the idea of Ashiya running such a tight ship in his own domicile unnerved her a little.

Ashiya's predeparture rundown continued on for several more minutes. At the end, they came to the agreement that Suzuno would provide all nonrice ingredients and cooking duties. It left her with mixed emotions; stuffing the demons full of Church-grade holy food usually filled her with glee—but the idea of them *asking* for it gave her pause. That, and something about using the Devil's Castle kitchen eliminated the "I slaved over this back at my place, so you *better* appreciate it" sense of superiority she relished.

"Oh… Leaving already, Ashiya?"

Suzuno's shouting was enough to wake up the yawning Maou, still half covered in the single sheet he slept under.

"Sure is cold this morning… Dang, 5:30 AM?! You're leaving *this* early?"

"I was asked to arrive at the Barres building on Shinjuku's west side by half past six. I figured the sooner I left, the better, just in case."

"…Well, I dunno where you're going, but good luck."

"Absolutely."

Maou had given Ashiya permission to take a few days off from his Devil's Castle duties, but for some reason Ashiya was reluctant to reveal either his destination or the exact nature of his new work.

He'd never quite managed to get it out of him. Ashiya stated that it was nothing illegal or physically dangerous, and that was good enough for Maou—although he couldn't guess why he had to meet up with someone this early in Shinjuku on a Friday. He pushed his blanket aside, stood up, and shivered a bit in his short-sleeved shirt.

"...I have already made breakfast," Suzuno flatly stated. "If you are that cold, warm up with some miso soup."

Looking over toward the kitchen, Maou saw a wooden-handled saucepan resting on one of the gas burners, steam rising out from it in the chilly air. "Whoa, nice," he said as he hurried up to it. Suzuno winced at the display, as Ashiya nodded approvingly at it.

"I am off, Your Demonic Highness. Please, whatever you do, keep an eye on Lucifer's behavior."

"Ahh, he'll be fine. Emi nearly killed him yesterday. I doubt he'll waste any more of our money... Not *this* month, anyway."

"No. Not this month."

Urushihara was cocooned in his own blanket like a baby moth, the picture of comfort as he softly snored.

"...Man, it really *is* cold."

"Perhaps. Oddly so, for the summer. Maybe it will rain later."

It had been an hour after they saw Ashiya off. The sun was now fully risen, but the temperature stubbornly refused to budge. Maou and Suzuno wouldn't have had any way of knowing it—owning neither a TV, nor a radio, nor a cell phone capable of receiving news stories—but a low-pressure front from mainland Asia was pushing away the warmer air from the Pacific, keeping temperatures low across metro Tokyo. The high temperature was eighty-six degrees Fahrenheit yesterday, but forecasters were calling for the mercury to stay in the sixties today. The cold still wasn't enough to awaken Urushihara, currently rolled up in a ball.

"Maybe I better go with long sleeves today," Maou murmured as he pulled out the plastic clothing bin that contained the demons' winter gear. "No need to go crazy with a sweater, but..."

Maou and Ashiya survived their first winter in Japan with layers. Lots and lots of layers. He wistfully recalled how they shopped for the thickest, cheapest gear they could find in order to avoid freezing to death, given that Devil's Castle lacked a suitable heater or even a futon to sleep on.

"Weird. I could've sworn I bought a Warm Tech shirt from Uni-Clo last year."

He and Ashiya both had a pair from UniClo's line of heat-trapping undergarments. But, try as he might, he couldn't find the shirt anywhere in the clothing bin.

"Are you *that* useless?" Suzuno asked with disapproving eyes. "Do you need Alciel to help you so much as find a single article of clothing?"

Maou averted his eyes.

"You are probably the type of person who forgets where you put your new socks after your old ones grow holes, aren't you?"

"Don't be stupid. We don't have any new socks here in the first place. Ashiya sews up any holes that pop up."

Urushihara turned over in his sleep behind them.

"...Is *that* how impoverished you are, Devil King?"

"Y'know," a testy Maou replied, "as a high-level Church cleric, I figured you people would have a little more compassion for the poor. If you're trying to save money, you have to get as much out of everything as you can."

Maou fumbled around another bin in the closet before fishing out a lightbulb encased in a cardboard sleeve labeled "20W." He took it out and handed it to Suzuno.

"Here, try shaking it."

"Huh...? It's broken, is it not? Did you forget to put it in the garbage?"

"Of course not. If you put this inside a sock, that makes it a lot easier to sew up any holes in it. You should try it when you get a chance."

Urushihara turned over on his side once again.

"I think it probably goes without saying that everything in Ashiya's sewing kit came from the hundred-yen shop, too..."

"Enough already." This was starting to sadden Suzuno. "Your shift begins in the afternoon, does it not? Do you require lunch?"

"If you could, thanks," Maou said as he carefully pushed the bulb back into its sleeve.

"...Very well. I've already prepared all the ingredients, so just tell me whenever you feel hungry. And wake up Lucifer already, would you?"

"Yeah, sorry."

Suzuno, having said everything she needed to, returned to her apartment. The moment the door closed behind her, she turned to the mirror stand facing her. She stared at her reflection, then fell to her knees, despondent.

"A Great Demon General, using a burned-out lightbulb to mend his socks..."

With Suzuno having mangled his bicycle a few days before, Maou was proceeding with his commute on foot for the time being. This meant he was starting to sweat a bit, even in the unseasonably cool weather, by the time he arrived at MgRonald. He guessed he'd be freezing again by the time night fell.

As evening approached, Chiho arrived for her own after-school shift, looking a little worried. "So," she asked, "did Ashiya leave already, or...?"

"Um? Yeah."

Maou had yet to explain to the girls what had gone on yesterday. But, mainly in order to keep Chiho from feeling guilty, the demons and Suzuno had a story concocted and ready for her.

"I wouldn't worry about him, though. He found himself a nice-paying temp gig, is all."

"A temp gig...?"

"Yeah. It's just, you know, after all that stuff with Sariel and Suzuno, he was kind of worried about leaving the two of us to ourselves, is all."

There was nothing false about that statement. He just omitted the fact that he was off to get Devil's Castle out of the red, not further into the black.

"Oh… I get it. So he'll be back in the evenings?"

"Uh, not quite. He's staying over for a few days…I guess?"

"Oh? What kind of work would need that from him?"

"Good question…"

Maou's vague response was not because he was hiding something. He honestly had no idea where Ashiya went. He knew that Ashiya worked short-term gigs like this now and then even after he'd gone full-time at MgRonald, but he didn't have a grasp of every place he went.

"All he said was, it's a job he never thought he'd take on as a Demon General."

That was a quote from their conversation in the hallway.

"Wow, what would that be? Something dangerous?"

"Nothing too dangerous, I don't think. Or illegal. Ashiya wouldn't do something that'd get us in trouble, anyway."

"True, yeah," Chiho said, her expression a little clouded at Maou's ambiguous answer. Maou decided to swiftly change the subject before she picked up on any other signals.

"Thing is, though, Urushihara is by himself in Devil's Castle right now. I'm a lot more worried about that! Like, what if he wastes more of our money, or leaves the gas on all day…?"

"Yeah…"

His cheerfulness did little to change Chiho's demeanor.

"But y'know," Maou began, trying a sterner approach as he patted Chiho on her shoulder, "I really don't think you need to worry much about us. If you're that concerned about Ashiya, feed him some home-cooked food when he's back, okay? He'll probably tell you all about it then."

"…Okay! I'll try to make something good for him."

The smile finally returned a little to Chiho's face. A subsequent mini rush of evening customers brought them both back to the hustle and bustle of work. It kept going steadily until nine PM, the end of Chiho's shift.

Maou wasn't entirely sure he cleared Chiho's mind of all doubt, but this would have to work for now. Even if she found out later, as long as Ashiya came back with forty thousand yen in hand, at least she wouldn't feel obliged to contribute any more to them. Foisting the responsibility for this on the shoulders of a high-school student would be a stain on his good name as Devil King.

Right now, all he had to do was hold down the fort with Urushihara.

"...And that's what I'm the most worried about," he muttered to himself as he walked the dark path back home, another Friday night shift in the books. As he expected, the night was brisk, an autumnal chill against his skin. Suzuno mentioned there'd be udon noodles waiting for him for dinner; it wasn't exactly a summer dish, but on a night like this, it'd actually kind of work. Maou found himself looking forward to it.

But what awaited him at home was the shock of his life.

"Um...what the hell is all this?"

The moment he stepped through the front door of his castle, his vision turned white. Greeting him was Suzuno, seated with a pained expression on her face, and Urushihara, racked with desperation. That, and—neatly arranged in front of them—an array of merchandise Maou had never seen before in his life: fresh fruit, what must have been several dozen bottles of kitchen cleaner, a newspaper dated today, and...

"...A brand-new fire extinguisher, five feather-bed futons, and a water filter in the sink."

"Wha... Wha... Wha...?"

"All told, about forty-five thousand yen, it seems."

Suzuno's voice sounded like the tolling of Death itself from beyond the grave.

✳

Chiho was seated on her bed, clutching a heart-shaped cushion as she made a call.

"…Oh, hey, this is Chiho. Sorry I'm calling you so late. Anyway, yeah, it sounds like he's gone out on a temp job of some kind… Right. He said he was staying on-site for it or whatever, so he's not gonna be back all that soon… Yeah, I know, right?"

Her expression was far from bright and cheerful as she spoke.

"Anyway, tomorrow's Saturday, so I'll make something up for them. It's the least I can do and all, so… All right. Talk to you later."

She ended the call, flung the phone down on the bed, then lay down and sighed.

"Maybe I was being mean to Urushihara after all."

✳

"Did… Did you buy all of that, Urushihara…?"

The fallen angel's shopping habits up to this point mostly revolved around computer accessories, snacks, and anything with sugar in it. Maou feared that the obsession was now spiraling into a mania of purchasing random objects for giggles.

"Dude, no!" Urushihara countered in an uncharacteristic panic. "You think I'd actually buy all this useful household crap?!"

"Okay, so what's going on, huh?! 'Cause none of this was here when I left this afternoon!"

"Calm down, Devil King."

Suzuno rose from her seat on the floor and thrust something that looked like a receipt in front of Maou's face.

"What's that? …Wait, a purchase order? One external hard drive…two thousand yen?"

"…Look, I know why Ashiya had to go out and work, okay?" Urushihara muttered, head tilted downward. "I know I can't pay it all back myself…but I figured I could pitch in a little, at least."

"It would appear," Suzuno interjected, "that Lucifer was a victim of acquisition fraud."

"Acquisition…fraud?" Maou's eyebrows arched at the unfamiliar term.

"Yes. When someone visits you, promising to purchase your

precious items, then forces you to sell them at fraudulently low prices."

"...Oh, yeah, I heard about that."

Maou had heard stories along those lines from the retirees he worked with during neighborhood volunteer cleanup duty. Mr. Watanabe, one of the regulars at his day job, mentioned some rumors about shady individuals going door-to-door with that scheme, mostly targeting older people and stay-at-home moms. The local neighborhood association had put a notice about it in their most recent newsletter.

"So you sold some kinda computer part to help pay back the forty thousand yen?"

"Yeah...but..."

"It would appear," said Suzuno, eyes uncommonly sympathetic for Urushihara's plight, "he came across a particularly cruel fraudster. It was a hard sell disguised as a purchasing service. By the time I realized something was amiss, it was already as you see here."

"Yeah, but...a newspaper subscription? The *fruit*, even?! What kind of rip-off artist sells everything from fruit to fire extinguishers?"

"I'm sorry. The fruit and newspaper were from other guys. I couldn't say no to 'em."

"Oh, *come* on." Maou fell to his knees. "What are you, stupid?! Just say you don't need that crap!"

"But, dude, they said they wouldn't leave unless I bought their stuff! Like, they said it was some kind of trial offer or something! They kept on jiggling the doorknob and stuff, and I didn't want them to break it or else we'd owe even *more* money!"

"That's exactly what they wanted you to think, man! They musta thought you were the most gullible person in the world!"

"Dude, I know, but they kept talking around me, no matter what I said. I couldn't get them to leave! They were really, like, convincing and stuff..."

Maou had to wonder what kind of talent it took to so thoroughly fleece a fallen angel and an alleged demon. Having never encountered a pitch like this, it was tough for him to picture.

"Devil King," Suzuno said, "there is no point berating Lucifer right now. No, not this supposed Great Demon General willing to fall for a newspaper-subscription pitch."

"Bell," Urushihara protested, "you're just rubbing salt in my wounds, okay?"

"The newspaper and fruit are fine. We can always have the subscription canceled, and the fruit was not that terribly expensive anyway. I would have said no," Suzuno said as she held a pear in the palm of one hand, "even if I saw this for half the price at the grocery store, but regardless..."

"I said quit it, Bell..."

"The problem is the other three items. Lucifer?"

"Oh. Uh...check this out, Maou," Urushihara said as he pointed at his computer screen.

"This website? 'Deluxe Life International Holdings'? What's with *that* convoluted name? It's a bunch of random English words strung together."

"That's the website of that sales outfit," Urushihara explained. "I tried calling the number they listed on there via SkyPhone."

"And?"

"Nobody picked up. I looked it up, and their HQ address is at a mixed-use office building in Tokyo. So I looked up their IP address, but the site's hosted on a rental server. I don't think their office PCs are connected to the Net."

"...So?"

"So, I mean, the extinguisher, the futons, the filter... I dunno if we can make 'em take those back. It's totally a bad company."

"Uh... Whoa. Wait a second. You said it was forty-five thousand yen total, right?"

Urushihara and Suzuno turned their faces away in tandem. The fallen angel didn't even have so much as a piggy bank to his name—any cash that wasn't in their shared bank account would have been in either Ashiya's or Maou's possession. In other words, whether he purchased this junk via credit or debit, that bank account would have already been charged.

"Ashiya's out working right now to make up for the *last* forty thousand," Maou grimly intoned. "And now look..."

Both he and Urushihara felt a cold shiver run down their spines. They were now another forty-five thousand yen in the hole—and it was flushed down the proverbial toilet.

"We gotta do something before he gets back."

"Yeah...or else he'll go on a demonic rampage!"

"He *is* a demon, yes," Suzuno added.

"Ashiya said he'd be back on Sunday night," said Maou.

"We gotta figure something out," Urushihara added, "or we may never see Monday morning."

"*We?* I didn't do anything wrong!" Maou exclaimed.

"I doubt Alciel would lend an ear to that excuse," Suzuno sadly retorted. "Truly, Devil's Castle has become a rudderless boat in his absence."

"Ugh! I knew it!!"

Maou's scream was enough to make the apartment walls shake.

✳

"This is it, huh...?"

Maou scoped out the tenant list on the front of the building. By sheer coincidence, the office building that housed Deluxe Life was within walking distance of Devil's Castle. He was expecting it somewhere downtown or in one of Tokyo's entertainment districts, but it was actually a dusty old building, nestled in anonymously among one of the thoroughfares that crossed the Koshu-Kaido road near Villa Rosa.

"Huh," he said to himself. "At least they aren't yakuza or anything."

Urushihara calling them a "bad company" kindled that possibility in his mind, but when he summoned his nerve and climbed up the stairs, he found a seemingly typical business space, with a metallic sign and reinforced glass doors forming an entryway. He could see a woman there, too. For Maou, who was here to demand the company issue a refund for the items they pushed on Urushi-hara, it was something of a relief.

He pulled the door open, which was enough to alert the receptionist of his presence.

"Good morning, sir. What can I help you with today?"

"Um," Maou began, "a salesman from your company visited us yesterday." He went on to explain the whole story to the front-desk lady—how they were approached by the salesman, how he wasn't personally at home at the time, how none of the merchandise had been used, and how badly he needed to return it.

"All right. This was over in Sasazuka then, sir? Give me just one moment while I find an agent for you, please."

The woman rose to her feet, took a thick manila folder out from a cabinet visible from Maou's seat, flipped through the pages for a little bit, then dialed an internal number on her phone.

"Hello, I have a return request at the front desk... All right. Certainly."

Putting the receiver down, she pointed out a pair of small couches on one side of the reception area. "One of our agents will be here shortly," she said. "Please, have a seat over there."

"Thanks."

This was going better than he thought. Maybe they didn't pick up Urushihara's phone call simply because they were a small company and ran out of free lines or something.

As Maou sat and waited, a man in a suit appeared from behind the reception desk. After exchanging a few words with the previous woman, he approached the other sofa. He was thin, bespectacled, and about the same size as Maou.

"Thanks for waiting! My name is Kuryu, and I'm the returns specialist for our retail division. You were Mister...Maou, correct?"

"Yes, sir..."

"And you'd like to return a...let's see here... Ah, a fire extinguisher, futon set, and water filter?"

"Right, yeah. That stuff."

Suddenly, Maou felt something ominous in the air. He had never given this Kuryu guy his name. Or, for that matter, specified the stuff Urushihara bought—er, was forced to buy. Was Devil's Castle the only sale they recorded all day yesterday?

The ominous feeling was quickly confirmed.

"Well, I hate to be the bearer of bad news…but I'm afraid we generally don't accept returns, sir."

"…What?"

"With the water filter in particular, when we installed it in your sink, we ran it once to test it out… I'm afraid we can't call that 'unused.'"

"Whoa, hang on a second! It was just once!"

That was the truth. Suzuno refrained from using the Devil's Castle sink once she found out about the fraud.

"I understand what you are trying to tell me, sir, but as the customer, you were witness to the entire installation process. The water filter is fully covered in our terms and conditions here."

"Terms…?!"

Kuryu handed Maou a sheet of paper he had never seen before.

"I don't remember seeing this yesterday," Maou said.

"We did hand it to you, sir. It's the responsibility of the customer to keep track of these things, so there's not much I can do about that…"

"How could I have lost it in a single day?"

"I'm afraid that's not something I can answer, sir," Kuryu said, deftly dodging the crux of Maou's bewildered question. "Also, I'm afraid we cannot accept the fire extinguisher, either."

"Huhh?!"

"Are you aware of the installation standards for those, sir?"

"Installation what?"

"Well, in an apartment building like yours, there need to be fire extinguishers in place within twenty meters of all entryways and stairwells—with the proper government-mandated labeling, and housed inside a specialized storage unit."

"R-right, but we've already got a common-use one out on the walkway…"

"Yes, but based on the size of your building, you'd be legally required to have at least two stationed on each floor. Twenty meters is the standard, but the exact positioning depends on the area the building occupies…and it would be against the law for us to remove a unit we've already installed."

Even if that was true, it wouldn't mean Maou was responsible as a tenant for covering those costs. Maou was quickly beginning to get the picture.

"Okay, what about the futons?"

"Well, if they're in unopened, unused condition, we can certainly accept those, sir. It was a set of seven feather-bed futons, correct?"

"…Um, that should be five."

"No, it was definitely seven. It's written right here, sir."

Kuryu then produced another sheet of paper, a copy of a sales slip with Urushihara's childlike signature on it. It resembled the receipt Maou saw at his apartment yesterday, but the printed part of it had a "7" next to the futon field instead of a "5."

"…I'm afraid that five futons wouldn't be a full set. If that's the case, even if they're unused, we'd only be able to refund the remaining five futons at their used-goods value."

In other words, they weren't interested in providing a refund from the get-go. They acted like legitimate sellers, then used a mixture of childish excuses and meandering logic to swindle their customers out of their money. And since nothing they sold was clearly defective in nature, they were counting on their victims to eat their losses and chalk it up as a lesson learned. Not even Maou could keep his cool any longer.

"…You're seriously gonna pull that act?"

"What do you mean, sir? You agreed to this entire transaction as our customer. We have the statement right here—and our goods weren't defective at all, I believe."

"That wasn't an agreement. That was a total rip-off! What kind of idiot would buy feather-bed futons in the dead of summer? Without any sheets, even?"

"...Sir, that 'idiot' was living in your place."

The tone of Kuryu's voice took a sudden nosedive. His face contorted itself into a threatening scowl.

"It was your side that agreed to the purchase in the first place. All we did was bring the merchandise to you. We didn't put a gun to your head and make you purchase it. I don't really see why you're complaining about it now. Nobody likes a whiner, you know."

"What?!"

Maou had lost his temper. Kuryu let it slide.

"It's no business of ours any longer, sir. We have a signed receipt, contract, and terms of service. The products aren't defective at all. If you still think we're ripping you off, then you're free to take us to court if you like. With all this documentation, we'd win handily, you realize—and after that, we could countersue you for filing a fraudulent complaint. That would also be a slam-dunk victory for us, and then you'd have to pay our court fees, you see. Are you still interested in trying that?"

"Damn...it..."

Nobody with this kind of attitude shift could possibly be a legit businessman. Even Maou, in his current agitated state, knew that even though Kuryu's argument seemed to make sense right now, it wasn't anything even close to the truth.

But he had no time to work with. It wasn't like he knew anything about the court system, and Ashiya would be back home before he'd have any chance to plead his case in front of a judge. Getting angry at this guy wouldn't accomplish anything for him because he wasn't interested in doing business at all. The man was a swindler. A devil in human clothing. And Maou could sit here and grit his teeth at him all he wanted, but with all his demonic force taken from him after the battle against Sariel, it was nothing Kuryu couldn't handle.

"Then, if we have an understanding, may I be excused?" the swindler asked. "I certainly don't mind calling the police if I have to."

Kuryu lifted himself off the sofa. The woman who had warmly greeted Maou earlier now had a hand on her phone receiver like a whip she was wielding to keep the lion at bay. Further discussion was clearly futile. If Maou left right now, that all but signaled his total defeat. But if he tried holding on any longer, they might call the police—or someone even more sinister, maybe. And right now, Maou was powerless. Just your typical young human.

"Go ahead! Call 'em if you want!"

Kuryu's and the receptionist's heads turned toward the voice... coming from the front door. Maou joined them, only to groan weakly at what he saw.

"...ugh."

"I'd be *more* than happy to see 'em here!"

The woman facing off against Kuryu now was Emi—someone who never should have been here in a million years.

"Um... Can I ask who you are?"

"Me? A defender of justice!"

"Huhh?" snorted Kuryu at Emi's completely heartfelt self-introduction.

"So? What'll you do? Call the cops, or not?"

"..."

Kuryu and the woman didn't move. Now it was Emi's turn to snort at them.

"I swear, with all the crap your company's pulling on people, I'm amazed you actually *want* the police to sniff around in here."

"Um... I don't know who you are, ma'am," said Kuryu, voice even deeper than when he verbally threatened Maou. "But if you keep messing with us, you'll have worse than the police to deal with. Get it?"

But this was nothing that could ever faze Emi. Maou had no idea what "worse than the police" meant, but assuming they were regular Japanese human beings, they'd have to employ an entire army base's worth of personnel and equipment to get on equal footing with the Hero.

"...So! As you can see, the moment I stepped in, this company starts threatening me. Did you get all that?"

The smartphone she had in her left hand had been shooting video the whole time. "Loud and clear," said the speaker—in Chiho's voice.

"What…!"

"So, are you calling the cops or not?" Emi grinned at Kuryu. "If you do, I'll give them a recording of everything you two said."

"…"

"Why are *you* here…?" asked Maou, speaking for everyone else in the room. She couldn't have been tailing him, he figured.

The stare-off between Emi and Deluxe Life continued for a few moments. Emi, to Maou's surprise, was the first to blink.

"…Right. Let's go."

"Huh?!" Maou's eyes bugged out of their sockets.

"Staying here any longer isn't gonna force them to deal with us. Let's just make them happy and leave."

"H-hey! Emi!"

The Devil King found himself having to scramble in order to catch up with her, already out the door. He could feel the dour glares from the Deluxe Life staff on his back as he did.

"S-Suzuno?!"

Suzuno was waiting for him outside the building. "When you're ready," Emi said, as if expecting her.

"Right."

The cleric entered the building, Emi and Maou behind her…and was back within a minute's time.

"Got it?"

"All set."

Maou stared dumbfounded at Suzuno.

"If you will allow me to summarize…"

"Uh?" Maou grunted.

"Emilia and Chiho saw right through your shallow intelligence."

"What?" Maou grunted. He looked to Emi for guidance. She gave him an awkward stare, then crossed her arms and turned her face to the side.

"At first I was just pissed off beyond imagining…"

"Erm?" Maou grunted.

"But…once I started thinking about why you went to the Tokyo City Hall building…like, without even thinking about anything…"

"Um, what? I can't hear you."

"…Ugh! Look! I hate to admit this—I really do—and I'm not convinced he bought that thing with that intention in the first place, either. But Lucifer saved my life in the end, okay? So I went over in order to thank him! And then I saw all that crazy junk in there…"

"Oh… So…"

"But anyway! It made me sick, the idea of owing you such a huge favor. If I didn't show you some kind of gratitude, it'd damage my name as a Hero! If I can succeed here, that'll be worth a hell of a lot more karma than your forty thousand yen, so we'll be even! You got that?!"

"Uh, I don't know how you're measuring karma here…but if you're gonna help me, then thanks. I'm glad for it."

"If…if you understand, then fine."

"Oh, hey, while you're getting all in my business, can I ask another favor?"

"I'm not getting 'all in your business'!" Emi began to blush. "I'm just paying you back! What is it?!"

Maou, to Emi's further chagrin, bowed his head deeply downward. "If this all works out in the end…don't tell Ashiya about any of it, all right? You too, Suzuno! When Ashiya starts talking about money, it gets scary, man!"

The request was clearly coming from the heart. It was not the kind of demand one would expect from the Lord of All Demons. Emi and Suzuno, taking in the full meaning behind it, each sighed an exasperated sigh.

✳

"Oh, welcome back. Are you okay, Maou?"

Back at the apartment, the group found Chiho manning the Devil's Castle computer.

"Y-yeah, I'm fine, but…Chi, why are you…?"

"Take a look at this first, Maou!"

"Huh?"

Chiho clicked the mouse button a few times.

"Are you aware of the installation standards for those, sir?"

"Whoa! That voice…?!"

It was Kuryu's low, rumbling growl. And the video was shot through the front glass doors, clearly showing both Maou's and Kuryu's respective faces.

"Yep. Got a great shot of it, no?" Emi proudly answered.

"Emi…" Maou shivered. "You didn't…"

"I heard the whole story from your 'in-home security guard' here," Emi promptly replied, cutting him off.

Urushihara, meanwhile, sat motionless on the floor, avoiding Maou's eyes and trying to fend off the humiliation.

"But you're short on time, right?" Emi continued. "We kinda took the direct approach because we needed to build an airtight case."

"But how'd you get that video…?" the Demon King asked.

"You've got the blessings of modern technology to thank for that. I used the SkyPhone app on my smartphone and saved the audio and video on your computer."

"SkyPhone…? You mean the phone app on Urushihara's notebook PC?"

"Yeah. I was a little worried since it's an old model, but no wonder you're glued to that thing every day. You got some nice equipment!"

SkyPhone was a program that made telephone calls with an Internet connection. Nowadays, even portable devices like smartphones could host and use apps like SkyPhone. While it depended on the circumstances of usage, usually as long as the device had camera capabilities, it was even possible to have video calling.

"Thanks for the…compliment?" groaned the unqualified "security guard."

"You're welcome. I actually meant it as one, for a change." Emi looked at the computer screen, one eyebrow arched.

"We spotted this, too," Chiho said as she clicked on an icon Maou didn't recognize. "Luckily, Urushihara doesn't keep his files very tidy on this computer. He's got his webcam set to auto-log mode, so there's still the video from yesterday showing the front of the apartment."

"Yeah, yeah, thanks for the compliment."

"I doubt she meant *that* as one," Suzuno said as both she and the equally computer-illiterate Maou sat in front of the screen.

"Wait, the one you bought earlier?" Maou said. He was referring to the webcam Urushihara bought and installed on his own volition, providing him with a feed of the outside world for reasons only he knew. It was monochrome and low-resolution, but it clearly showed the street that crossed by the Devil's Castle window. A commercial van appeared to have parked, and a man in a suit jumped out from the passenger side.

"Whoa, that's Kuryu!"

The so-called returns specialist was busily removing a futon and a fire extinguisher from the back of the van.

"So basically," Emi explained, "this guy set out to rip you off from the very beginning. He claimed he was buying things from you, but that was just a cover story for what he was *really* doing, and that's all subject to government regulations."

"Is it...?"

"They're required by law to tell you from the start what the purpose of their visit is—solicitation, sales, purchasing, whatever. This video's pretty ample evidence that they were here from the start in order to sell you stuff—not buy it from you, like they claimed. Too bad we can't see the license plate from this angle...but if we can see his face this clearly, that oughta be more than enough."

"Yeah, but how come you know all of that?" Maou pleaded.

"Well, there's a ton of regulations we have to follow doing business over the phone," Emi explained, obviously detailed on the subject. "I'm more involved with fielding questions than actively soliciting sales, but they cover all that in our job training anyway."

"Ah, Japan certainly does make things convenient," an astonished Suzuno remarked. "Imagine, someone leaving such a clear trail of evidence to follow! A shame it never went so easy with the corrupt regional bishops and businessmen of the Western Island!"

"Right," Urushihara interjected, "but Yusa, isn't it, like, against the law to take hidden-camera footage and stuff without permission? Like, you're not allowed to use it as evidence or something like that?"

"No," Chiho replied as she watched the screen, "but that's just talking about whether it's admissible in court or not. That, and *this* video is surveillance, not a hidden camera—it's not meant for illegal activity or invading people's privacy or anything. And if it's this bad of a company, even if it can't be evidence, it's still enough for the police to start an investigation with "

"You really are a policeman's daughter, aren't you?" said Emi, impressed at the mature knowledge Chiho was spouting.

"Oh, it's really nothing that complicated. But I was wondering about something else, though." She turned toward Urushihara, a little bashful. "How old are you, Urushihara?"

"Huh?" he asked back.

"Um, like, not in demon or fallen-angel years… Here in Japan, I mean."

"Oh, right, what did I put him down as…?"

Urushihara looked up at the (on paper, anyway) head of the Devil's Castle household. The name "Hanzou Urushihara" was one thought up by Maou once it became clear they would have to live together in Sasazuka.

"I think I put him down as eighteen. He's such a child, so…"

Maou and Urushihara, and Ashiya for that matter, all had to craft a full set of government-approved documents backing up their identities in order to pass as Japanese citizens. They forged them with a mixture of social engineering and demonic power-driven hypnosis. Without a presence in the government family register, after all, they'd be unable to do much of anything in this country.

"He *is* a child," Emi echoed.

"Indeed," Suzuno added. "Far, *far* less mature than Chiho, even."

This news significantly brightened Chiho, however. "Oh! So you're still a minor, Urushihara," she chirped with a smile.

"Oh, right," Emi said, nodding. "The cooling-off period and all that, huh?"

"Right!"

"What? I don't have AC here."

"No, cooling *off*," Emi explained to the clueless Demon King beside her. "Basically, it's a system where you can unconditionally cancel a sales contract or request within a certain period of time. With door-to-door sales in particular, people sign on the dotted line before they know what they're doing a lot of the time, so it's kind of a safety valve for consumers. The cooling-off system's even stronger for minors, though. If their guardian says, 'I didn't agree to that' within that period of time, they can cancel pretty much any kind of contract, just like that. This happens a ton of the time when minors sign stuff like cell phone contracts."

As Emi put it, high school–age teens would occasionally forge their parents' permission on DokoDemo contracts, leading to consternation down the line.

"Have you ever looked at the bottom part of a résumé form, Maou?" Chiho asked. "There's usually a little bit there saying that minors need permission from a parent or guardian in order to seek work."

"Oh, yeah, you're right…"

It had been a fair amount of time since he last filled out a Japanese-style résumé form, but he recalled that was one of the sections he left empty on it.

"I had to get that filled out, since taking a part-time job involves a full work contract and everything. This one isn't exactly like that, but regardless, a minor always needs the permission of a guardian in order to sign a contract that involves more money than they're permitted to have."

"But I'm not exactly Urushihara's dad, you know? We've got separate family registers and everything."

"Yeah, dude, I like you and all, but..."

"Having *you* as my son would be hell on earth," Maou fired back.

"Right," Emi cut in, "but you work to support that shut-in freak, don't you? In that case, it'd probably be easy for you to declare yourself his legal guardian."

"Uh, what did you call me, Emilia?"

Emi ignored him.

"And he spent forty-five thousand yen of yours, didn't he? I really doubt you're giving Lucifer that much of an allowance. That's got to be more than what he can work with by himself, so I think the cooling-off period can apply to this contract."

Maou's expression, dark and troubled before Emi began speaking, was starting to brighten. If all of this legal mumbo jumbo meant Ashiya wouldn't be raging at him in a couple days, he was all but ready to worship Emi and Chiho as goddesses.

"Wow, so do you think I could use that cooler thing to return that transmitter he bought, too?"

"*Cooling off*, all right? And no, probably not, if he bought it online. That was on *your* card, I imagine, so you're on the hook for that. You looked at the thing before you bought it, right? Unless it's unopened or defective or something, I doubt you can return that unconditionally."

"Oh..."

This was a slight disappointment for Maou.

"That device saved both me and Yusa, though," Chiho said, standing up from her station and walking in front of Urushihara. "I'm sorry about earlier, all right? You saved the day for both of us, but I said some really mean things to you."

"...It wasn't me, dude," Urushihara said, dipping his head awkwardly to the side. "Maou's the guy who saved you."

"Maybe, but if it wasn't for you, Maou might not have reached us in time. Emi and I were actually thinking that we should contribute some of the money for that tracker, but..."

"Whoa, really?!"

The unexpected confession made both Maou and Urushihara look at Emi. She turned away, clearly peeved. "That cheap bum Alciel never breathed a word of it to us," she muttered. "I'm sure he'd never accept the money. Besides," she continued, eyes firmly upon Uru-shihara, "I know it saved our hides in the end, but I know you didn't put the tracker in my bag for any *decent* reason, Lucifer. I figure you owed me one for that, and I made up for it by kicking your ass yesterday. But on the other hand, I'm partly at fault for getting Chiho involved, so I wanted to help make up for your loss a little, too...and Chiho agreed to join me on that. Does that make sense now?"

It was fairly convoluted logic, but what it meant was that both Emi and Chiho had come to Maou and Urushihara's aid today. For now, that was good enough.

"Well!" said Maou, indicating his tacit approval by changing the subject. "At least I know we've got a chance. But what should we do with that info? Call the cops?"

Emi and Chiho shook their heads. "There's nothing illegal about the paperwork itself," Emi explained. "Even if we went through the cops, they'd never get it settled before Alciel comes back. Not unless this was a seriously huge rip-off scheme."

"Great. So now what?"

"How about this?"

Chiho returned to the computer and brought up another website. It had the name of another outfit unfamiliar to Maou.

"The Tokyo Department of Consumer Affairs?"

✳

Said department, located in the Iidabashi section of Shinjuku ward, served as the main Tokyo corporate body in charge of consumer complaints. It was open on Saturdays. Maou immediately headed off to complain about Deluxe Life International Holdings and was soon greeted by a so-called consumer counselor who listened to the entirety of his story.

The counselor, a gentle-voiced man named Mr. Tamura, explained to him that his department had received several complaints about Deluxe Life in the past, but Maou was the first victim to bring such crystal-clear evidence of their activity to their attention.

"We'll get in contact with this company at once," he said. "I don't think you have anything left to worry about, Mr. Maou."

It was exactly the kind of reassurance Maou wanted to hear, as Mr. Tamura picked up the phone and made calls to several people. Then:

"Well, that was a close call. They almost got away from us."

"Huh?"

"With the contract your friend signed, Mr. Maou, that would have been easy for us to cancel using the normal cooling-off regulations. But, just in case, I sent our weekend agent over in Shibuya and our affiliated judicial partner to the site. It turns out they arrived just as those frauds were trying to ditch the office and leave. There was a moving truck by the front door and everything."

"Ditch the office...?"

"It's a common trick," Mr. Tamura said, unfazed. "They take out the computer equipment and other records first, send the desks and lockers and things to recycling agents, and then they run away. If they were well prepared for it, they could clean out your typical one-floor office and set up shop somewhere else within half a day's time. I'm sure you're far from their only victim, Mr. Maou."

Maou found it all a little too hard to imagine. As far as he could tell, Deluxe Life had a perfectly legitimate-looking office setup. Without the aid of demonic force, he figured it must have taken a lot of people to construct and take down an entire office in such a short time, but it was hard to believe so many people could be involved in what amounted to a ring of criminals.

"It doesn't take a lot of skill to run a group like this, actually. I sincerely doubt anything like organized crime was involved with them. If it was, I'd imagine they've long since cut ties with a small-time operation like that. Also, I'm happy to report that they found the

contract signed by Mr. Urushihara as well. He had made the purchase via bank card, but they didn't even have their own card
processor, so the contract was still in their to-do pile. They never
reported it to the bank, so I don't think your card was ever debited at
all. Lucky break there, huh?"

If Emi and Chiho were goddesses, then Mr. Tamura was the only
Supreme Being Maou was willing to accept right now.

"By the way, though, it was apparently a rather odd scene at their
office. The staff was trying to run away, but for some reason they
couldn't open the door or windows in their own office. When our
agent arrived, one of the movers was attempting to break a window
open for them."

"They couldn't open them...?"

Come to think of it, Suzuno spent a moment or two inside there
after he left. It kind of seemed as if Emi had given her the signal to
do...something. Perhaps she put some manner of sealing magic over
the building to keep them from escaping. Maou could only guess at
the exact nature of it.

"Either way, I'm sure their business license will be revoked before
too long...although I'm sure they'll find a way to file for bankruptcy
and try the scheme over again somewhere else."

Mr. Tamura's eyes grew stern.

"Mr. Maou, we managed to get you out of trouble this time. There's
no doubt that this company actively attempted to victimize you and
your friend. But like we've seen with all the identity theft going on,
these thieves are always going to find another way to trick people.
Most of the complaints we received for this outfit were from elderly
people, but you're still a young man. There's no saying you'll be this
lucky next time. So try to be a little more careful, all right?"

For once in his over three-hundred-year-old life, Maou had no
complaints about being called young. To someone like him, experienced with holy power–wielding Ente Islans like Emi and Suzuno
as well as with honest-minded Earthlings like Chiho and his boss
Kisaki at work, it was a surprise for him to realize that people in

Japan could even be so ill-minded and deceptive. Even for a Devil King like him, there was still so much to learn.

"I'll do my best," he said, bowing. "Thanks a ton for all your help. Speaking of which…"

Ever since he set foot in this facility, something had been nagging on his mind.

"Do we, uh, owe you anything for interceding on our behalf?"

Mr. Tamura smiled and shook his head. "Visitors have to incur fees sometimes if we need to get attorneys or judicial agents involved, but this was an open-and-shut case for us, so you're fine for today. It's your taxes that keep the lights on in here, after all. If you run into any other trouble, don't be afraid to contact us again, all right?"

The municipal tax deducted from Maou's already paltry paycheck was usually a source of stress to him. For the first time in his human life, he actually felt glad he was required to pay it.

＊

"I definitely wanna invite Tamura the counselor guy into my army someday."

"Don't be stupid."

The gang was back inside the now much emptier Devil's Castle. Emi was once again resuming callously shooting down the Devil King's latest grand scheme.

Not long after Maou returned home, Kuryu paid them another visit—this time accompanied by the consumer affairs agent covering Shibuya ward. He had come to take back the futons, fire extinguisher, and water filter.

"Nothing to worry about," Mr. Tamura said when Maou decided to call him before letting Kuryu inside. "That's exactly the kind of caution I was talking about. That's good. Keep up the good work."

For all the bluff and bluster Kuryu gave Maou earlier in the afternoon, he was almost eerily friendly with him now that the agent was watching his every move. The documents were formally annulled in Maou's presence, the head of the local newspaper office came to apologize after Maou called to complain, and the threat to Devil's Castle (and the threat of Maou's and Urushihara's grisly murders at Ashiya's hands) was finally quashed for good.

"Thank you all so much! Emi, Chi, Suzuno... I owe all of you one! Hey, Urushihara!"

"Yeah...uh, thanks, I guess—*Yeow!*"

"Bow your head, dumbass!"

He pushed his head down, dissatisfied with the token gratitude Urushihara had to offer.

"Y-you don't have to go that far," a harried Chiho said with a smile. "I'm just glad we could help out."

"The fruit's still gonna be your problem, though," Emi said. "Gotta pay for your mistake somehow, you know?"

"Yeah, you said it."

The pears cost a total of a thousand yen or so. Maou decided to keep them around, as a sort of cautionary tale for all of them.

"You girls want any?" he asked.

"No thanks. They look kind of old anyway."

"Um, I'm okay, too, thanks."

"See?" Suzuno sneered. "I told you they were asking too steep a price for that quality. You had best eat them all before Alciel returns, lest you incite his rage for quite different reasons."

Following her advice, Maou peeled one of the pears, probably not the stuff of organic boutique farmers, and took a bite.

"I can't believe people actually do that, though," he whispered as he savored the less than succulent flavor.

"You think it's that rare? You *are* the King of All Demons, right?"

"Yeah, but demons don't pull underhanded BS like that," Maou said, Kuryu's face crossing his mind. "We don't really have the concept of 'wheeling and dealing,' y'know? We like to keep our evil on the simple side. Something like that... A guy smiling at you as he tightens the noose around your neck... I didn't know that existed."

"You see?" Suzuno scoffed. "Not all humans are good people,

indeed. As a Church cleric, I know that all too well...but I am also duty bound to treat all lives as equal. If that Kuryu gentleman was killed by the demons that marauded Ente Isla...then he would be the victim, one who needed to be saved. A thorny dilemma, and one I still have trouble coming to grips with."

Her voice had tapered to a whisper toward the end. Then, realizing something, she lifted her head back up.

"But...but this does *not* mean I see logic or justice in *your* evil ways! Do not misinterpret my meanderings!"

"Yeah, yeah," Maou snickered to himself.

"You wonder where people go wrong, though," Chiho glumly observed. "We're all innocent when we're born, you know."

"No telling," Maou replied. "But people make mistakes all the time, yeah? Some people put up sham companies like that, and other people keep tabs on them. Like Mr. Tamura and that Shibuya agent, y'know? Weird place, this human world... The demon realms're a lot easier to deal with."

"Yeah. I'll definitely give you that."

For once, Urushihara actually agreed with something Maou said.

The group decided to commemorate surviving their brush with financial death with a special dinner that night, complete with pork cutlets from the neighborhood butcher provided by Suzuno. Maou had work from Sunday morning on, and after strictly warning Urushihara to lock the door and pretend he wasn't there, he set off and ran through his shift, thanking Chiho once again when she arrived.

They both got off at six PM, with Chiho once again offering some home-cooked food for the night's dinner. And when the two of them arrived at Devil's Castle:

"Whoa! You're back, Ashiya?!"

"Welcome, Your Demonic Highness!"

Ashiya was already home.

"Ashiya! Welcome back!"

"M-Ms. Sasaki?!"

Chiho's presence was clearly a shock to him. Suzuno gave his shoulder a quick pat.

"Chiho knows you went out to make back that forty thousand yen. Give it up."

"Wh-what? Is that true…?"

"Thanks for all your hard work, Ashiya. Earning back the money that saved my life and everything…"

"No, it…it was nothing, really…"

"Oh, it's all right," Chiho reassured him. "Maou gave me the whole story, so at least let me express my gratitude to you and Urushihara, okay?"

Chiho's food container contained, amazingly enough, three eel filets done up *kabayaki* style, broiled in a soy-based sauce. She couldn't have fished them out of some river; presumably they were bought somewhere, and by the looks of them, they couldn't have come cheap.

"Hey, I gotta do this much for you, at least," Chiho insisted. The three demons, beaten down by the display, gladly accepted the feast.

"So what kind of work were you involved in?" Chiho asked over the dinner table.

Ashiya's face darkened a bit. "It pains me to say it," he began, bowing his head down a bit as he began his confession, "but I was an instructor…"

"An instructor?!"

Maou, Urushihara, and Suzuno were equally surprised to hear the word.

"Yes. At an overnight camp run by a test-prep center."

This struck the entire room dumb.

"But I wasn't at the whiteboard teaching students. I was a conversational partner, helping them with English pronunciation and listening skills."

"Oh, that sort of thing?"

Maou nodded. It made enough sense to him. He didn't know what Emi's experience was, but he and Ashiya had mastered the Japanese language without the use of demonic force in the space of a few days. They had kept up the language study for a while longer, figuring it would help both of them get salaried positions somewhere, but apparently Ashiya was at the point where he could get work as an English instructor.

"Lo, I am a Great Demon General…and, *ohh*, how it pains me to use my powers to train mere human beings. But we need to stay afloat!"

"That is…one way of putting it, perhaps," a confused Suzuno said.

"Aw, it's fine, isn't it, Ashiya?" Maou asked.

"…Huh?"

"If you're instructing them," Maou went on to the demon man's surprise, "I doubt those kids are gonna go wrong. If you can get a stint there again, I say take it."

"Um? Er, all right," Ashiya replied quizzically. "I doubt it will happen that often, my liege." Then he turned to Urushihara. "Lucifer! Did anything happen to His Demonic Highness?"

"Not really, no," came the reply, the fallen angel too brazenly focused on his eel filet to look at him. "Just the same goofball as always." But instead of leaving it at that, he raised his head up, a grain of rice still stuck to his cheek.

"Oh, but…"

"Hmm?"

"Ashiya, you fight some seriously rough enemies in this joint, don't you?"

"Huh?"

"He's got a point, Chi," Maou observed to the side. "Nothing but honest business for us, though, right?"

Chiho smiled and nodded. "You said it!"

"Stupid Devil King," Suzuno whispered. "As if he has any room to speak." As usual, it disappeared into the air unnoticed as the meal between demons, holy women, and one normal teenage girl continued.

✳

Emi, finally at her home in Eifukucho after a particularly annoying Sunday shift, took a peek at the clock. *Alciel must be home by now,* she thought.

Considering how she had just spent the weekend, it began to seem slightly ridiculous to her that out of everybody in Villa Rosa Sasazuka right now, the only phone number she had was the Devil King's. Slaying him was supposed to be her main priority, not sharing digits with him. If Suzuno was planning to stay on Earth for a while to come, Emi thought she should probably try to convince her to buy a mobile phone of her own.

As she pondered over this, her door intercom beeped at her.

"Yes?" she said, speaking into the receiver. The intercom screen displayed the scene in the lobby of her apartment building. It showed a man, a Westerner, with a serene smile on his face. In his hand was a small, leather-bound book.

Emi, watching the man take a breath, didn't like where this was going. She was right to feel that way.

"Hello! I was just wondering if you have accepted God into your—"

"I'm fine, thanks!!" Emi screamed as she slammed the intercom's receiver back on the wall. Good lord, indeed. Between door-to-door salesmen assaulting Devil's Castle and religious zealots hounding the Hero of the Holy Sword herself, there was never any letting one's guard down in this country.

"Let's take a shower," Emi angrily declared to nobody in particular as she stormed off, seeking to put the stress of the workday and entire weekend behind her.

THE DEVIL PLUCKS A
CAT OFF THE STREET

A rogue cloud had chosen that certain day in midsummer to park itself over greater Tokyo and give the metropolis a little relief from the sun. Cracking the window open brought a pleasant breeze inside, keeping things amply comfortable within the main room.

However, that wasn't strictly necessary because the gaps in the plastic sheeting they were using to cover the gigantic hole in the wall let in air on a fairly constant basis.

But beyond those light flapping noises, all was quiet this evening. And Shirou Ashiya, known—nay, feared—as "the Great Demon General Alciel" in another world, could sense that his master was back. He could hear it in the squeal of the brakes attached to Dullahan II, the two-wheeled steel horse his overlord commuted to work on. It was followed by the ruffle of him placing a cover over it, followed by hesitant steps up the common-use stairway, making sure he had ample traction at every pace.

Wiping off his clothes, Ashiya took a couple of steps toward the front door to greet his master. The door opened, and…

"…My liege."

There stood Devil King Satan, aka Sadao Maou in this world—Ashiya's master, the leader of all able-bodied monsters of the demon realms, who once led his armies on a quest to conquer the land of

Ente Isla and turn it into an all-inclusive resort for himself and his slavering peoples. He looked no older than his early twenties at most, and none of the awe-inspiring figure he once cut as Devil King remained. Were you to infuse his now-human body with a little demonic power, however, he would instantly regain his true, fearsome guise, capable of freezing mere mortals on the spot and sending them into paroxysms of despair.

And inside the pocket of his well-worn UniClo jacket, he was carrying something that Ashiya had a little trouble comprehending at first.

"...*Meee*," it weakly cried as Maou fully removed it from his pocket—a kitten with a silvery sheen to its hair.

"..."

"..."

Master and servant spent the next few moments staring at each other by the front door. Somehow, the master looked quite a bit more apologetic than the servant.

"I, uh," he meekly began, "it was shivering by the grease bin, so..."

"Take it back to where you found it, please," Ashiya promptly protested.

"You demon!"

"So I am. What of it?"

"Ehhh-*choo*!"

The third occupant of the apartment—Hanzou Urushihara, known and not at all feared as the fallen angel Lucifer in their home world—sneezed loudly, startling the kitten in Maou's hands.

※

The next morning, Suzuno Kamazuki—the next-door neighbor to Devil's Castle, known on Ente Isla as high Church cleric and Reconciliation Panel board member Crestia Bell—found herself puzzled by an unfamiliar sound.

"...What is that?"

It sounded like the wailing of some animal, likely a cat, and it sounded frightfully close to her.

The Villa Rosa Sasazuka apartment building had a back-alley space lined by concrete-brick walls, a rarity in this day and age. It was a favorite hangout spot for stray cats across the neighborhood, but ever since she'd moved in, Suzuno didn't remember hearing any catfights within earshot of her apartment, and something about the grass in the backyard lawn seemed to deter their occasional visitors from relieving themselves all over it.

Confused, Suzuno got up off her futon, changed into her everyday kimono, put the futon away in the closet, and began cooking breakfast. The meowing continued uninterrupted the entire time. She took a peek out the kitchen window. There was nothing too cat-shaped within sight. Maybe some stray had given birth to kittens inside the walls or something. It was a bit out of season for that, but anything was possible.

There was a knock on the door. "Bell?" a familiar voice asked. "It's me. Sorry for visiting so early."

"Emilia? What is it?" Suzuno asked, wiping her hands on her apron as she walked to the door.

"Hey, sorry to bother you. I needed to deliver something."

"Deliver?"

Beyond the door, carrying a paper bag, was the Hero of Ente Isla, Emilia Justina, currently calling herself Emi Yusa because of reasons too numerous to get into here.

"Eme sent me a little extra holy energy drink, so I thought I'd freshen your supply a little."

"Well! I thank you."

Holy energy powered the magical skills that had safely ferried Emi and Suzuno through untold dangers up to this point. Unlike in Ente Isla, however, their bodies could not generate this force by themselves on Earth. It was thanks to the bottles of 5-Holy Energy β sent on regular occasions by Emi's former traveling partner, Emeralda Etuva, that the two girls could still tap their magic.

"Are you leaving for work next?"

"No," a depressed-looking Emi said as she looked at the next door over. "Today's a scheduled playdate with Alas Ramus's 'daddy.'"

"…"

It was enough to peeve Suzuno into silence as well, before she noticed that a certain important part of that playdate was missing.

"Where is Alas Ramus herself?"

"…She was looking forward to it so much, she got up before dawn and wound up falling asleep again."

Emi tapped her forehead for illustration.

The holy sword fused within the Hero Emilia's body had been further infused with the presence of Alas Ramus, a shard from one of the Sephirot jewels that formed seeds for new worlds within Ente Isla's heavens. She had taken the form of a toddler in this world, and for reasons nobody could fathom, she thought the Devil King and Hero were her father and mother, respectively.

Since bonding with Emi, Alas Ramus was no longer able to venture far from "Mommy" by herself. She still missed "Daddy," however, and so Emi was forced to take her "daughter" on visits to Devil's Castle on regular occasions. Otherwise, the child would bawl at her inside her brain, wailing in a voice only she could hear. It didn't do much for her continued sanity.

Having Alas Ramus present only within her mind was convenient at times—it saved on day-care costs, for one—but Emi figured that keeping her in her own toddler body was probably the best thing from a child-raising perspective. It distressed Suzuno, however. The idea of Emi being forced to deal with the Devil King like a single mother dealing with a dual-custody divorce wasn't anyone's idea of a happy time.

"Aahh-*choo*!!"

Both of the girls shivered a bit at the sudden elephantine roar.

"…That was Lucifer, wasn't it?"

Emi winced. The sneeze had neatly swept away the refreshing morning atmosphere.

"What's going on in there, anyway? It sounds like they're having a party or something."

The furor surrounding Alas Ramus's arrival on Earth had ultimately led to a large hole being poked in the wall of Villa Rosa Sasazuka Room number 201. The sheet they used to cover it didn't block sound leaking through to the adjacent apartment even on the best of days, but today was turning into a particularly loud one.

"I don't know," Suzuno replied. "That act has continued anon since morning. Perhaps the chill air made him catch cold overnight."

Neither the Hero's nor the Church cleric's tone indicated they cared that much about the demons' physical health. But the next sound made both of them exchange curious glances.

"*Meww!!*"

"Huh?"

It was that cat again, the same one Suzuno had been listening to since she woke up. They were still trying to grasp the situation, but it sounded like it was only getting worse on the other side of the paper-thin wall. Before long, they could hear all three of them—the Devil King, the Demon General, and the fallen angel— like they were in the same room.

"Dah! I lost him! Grab him, Urushihara!"

"Dude, I can't! Whoa, stay away from me! Nnnaaahh-*choo!*"

"How…how dare you defy us, you puny animal! Come here at once!"

"*Mee! Meee! Mewwww!!*"

"What is going *on* in there?"

Emi couldn't guess why there was a cat in Devil's Castle, but from what she could hear, this new pet wasn't exactly a marvel of domestic obedience.

Another few moments, and—

"…Whew! Finally gotcha, you little sneak! Who's your master now, huh?!"

"*You're* the one who let him jump out of your lap, my liege."

"Dude, would you *please* just do something about him already— ah, ahh-*choo!!*"

"Do you think…!"

Emi and Suzuno gave each other another look. The same thought had popped into both of their minds. Right now, Maou and his cohorts were, to put it charitably, in a distressed financial state. They still seemed adamant about following the social norms of Japan and finding a legitimate way to eke out a bare livelihood, but they definitely had little in the way of wiggle room right now.

Were Maou and his demons about to commit one of the greatest taboos Japanese urban culture had to offer? Trapping stray animals on the street and using them to stave off their hunger? The image in Suzuno's mind was, at least, quite a bit more demonic than the way they had been acting up to now. There was no way Devil's Castle could support anything like a house pet at the moment—and none of its residents had ever demonstrated interest in the idea until now.

It took the tandem image of Maou, in demon form, chewing on a kitten's skull for both Suzuno and Emi to hurry out the door.

"Devil King!!" bellowed Suzuno in front of the Room 201 door, taking out her hairpin and deploying the Light of Iron magic. The moment she did, it transformed into a massive warhammer, one that could easily tear the entire apartment building down to its bare frame.

"S-Suzuno?!" Maou shouted.

"Open this door at once, Devil King! I refuse to allow this tragedy to continue any further! Feasting on the poor, homeless animals of this city…and yet you dare call yourself a king?!"

"N-no! What are you… Geez, keep it down…!"

"Open up! Release the cat at once!"

Suzuno jiggled the doorknob, ignoring Maou's protests. It was locked.

"I'm going in, Bell!" Emi shouted as she returned to Suzuno's room and leaned out her window. She was actually trying to make it into Devil's Castle by shimmying across the outer wall. If any passersby saw her, a police visit would seem pretty likely.

"Face thy divine punishment!!" With a mighty roar, Emi made it across and through the window to Devil's Castle.

"Whoa! E-Emi?! How'd *you* get in?!"

There, seated on the ground, was Sadao Maou, holding a kitten.

"Shut up! How could any Devil King capture and consume a poor, innocent stray cat?! That's just pathetic!"

Emi raised her sword of justice into the air, took a deep breath as she mentally prepared to stop this great injustice, then noticed something.

"All right!" Maou shouted. "I see it now! You've got the wrong idea, okay? But this guy's finally chilled out and everything! Keep quiet for a sec!"

She was all but expecting to come in and see Filet-O-Cat in the frying pan. Instead she was looking at Maou trying to get a feeding syringe into the kitten's mouth, Ashiya trying frantically to get some sticky, sweet-smelling white powder off the floor, and Urushihara sitting in a corner, watery-eyed and rubbing the reddened tip of his nose.

"What...are you...?"

Emi had trouble parsing all of it at once.

"Is it not *obvious*?!" a peeved Ashiya shouted, rubbing a wet washcloth against the floor.

"Um," Emi answered, holy sword still thrust into the sky. "You were trying to give milk to that kitten, it jumped out of your lap and knocked over the powdered milk container, and now you're trying to syringe-feed him? ...Maybe that?"

She had a decent hunch she was right.

"If you can see that, then get out of here!" Ashiya screeched. "We do not have the time to deal with you right now!"

"Ashiya, inside voice, okay? You're gonna make him panic again... Oh, I think he's having some."

The silvery kitten in Maou's hands, finally admitting surrender, began nursing on the cap of the feeding syringe.

"There we go! See? Just be a good cat and drink up, and there's nothing to be scared of! Eesh..."

Maou continued to gripe as he pushed down on the plunger, making sure none of the milk spilled out of his patient's mouth.

"Awesome. We're done. Okay, back you go!"

He then placed the kitten back inside a fairly large cardboard box in another corner of the room.

"Um...so what's that kitten about, anyway? You're really not gonna eat him?"

"...Look, Emi, who do you think we are, anyway?"

"Demons?"

"Indeed, my liege."

"Yeah, I—ahhh-*choo!*"

The sneezing seemed to be gaining in volume. It was drowned out by a pounding on the door.

"Emilia! Emilia, what is happening in there? I demand to know! Tell me!"

"I'm up way too early for this crap," Maou whined as he rushed to the door before it got knocked off its hinges.

"M-my liege, watch where you—!!"

Ashiya's warning came an instant too late for Maou to avoid stepping right on the milk powder he hadn't wiped up yet. He groaned in defeat.

Maou, realizing the need to placate the still-suspicious Suzuno, decided it was high time to explain the events of the previous night to the two human girls.

"So you know how cold it was overnight last night, right? I figured a little guy like this would die out there unless he had some shelter 'n' stuff. There wasn't anyone else I could take him to back there, either, so... It's just human decency, you know, Alas Ramus?"

"Meow Meow!"

His eyes were pointed at the child seated in Emi's lap.

Emi swinging her holy sword around Devil's Castle was enough to wake Alas Ramus up, but the sight of the kitten made any annoyance at the rude awakening quickly forgotten.

"Meow Meow! Meowwwww? Lemme look!"

It took a herculean effort from Emi to keep the intensely curious

Alas Ramus from running right up to the box. *Restraint* wasn't in her dictionary yet, which could leave either her or the kitten or both with scars, so Emi decided to err on the side of caution.

"Don't talk to me about human decency, you," an irritated Emi growled as she played an ever-evolving game of grab-the-toddler with Alas Ramus.

"But," Suzuno said as she peered into the box, her hair already set back in place, "perhaps we should not blame him."

Inside the simple, towel-lined shelter was a small, furry ball of silver, his tiny legs propelling him as he sniffed around the walls. Sometimes he would dart his nose into a corner, seeking to answer some question only he could perceive; sometimes he would stop dead and stare at an empty point in the air. It was completely unpredictable, and every move was more endearingly cute than the last one.

"Your mouth's open, Suzuno."

"Agh!!"

Suzuno, enthralled, snapped out of it and looked back up.

"Hmph," Ashiya snorted, taking care of the last of the spilled powder. "The high and mighty Church cleric rendered dumb by such a juvenile sight. Why, how are you any different from Alas Ramus, I ask?"

Suzuno ignored him, cheeks flushed. "Well," she grumbled at Maou, "at least I know you are unwilling to prey upon defenseless animals for your nefarious schemes, at the very least."

"Come on."

"Daddy! No eating Meow Meow!"

Maou rolled his eyes at the both of them. "See? Now you got Alas Ramus thinking I'm the villain here."

"…I apologize. But!" Suzuno paused for breath, looking around at Devil's Castle, arranged identically to her own room. "What do you intend to do with it? Villa Rosa Sasazuka explicitly bans pets from the premises."

"…Yeah, about that."

Judging by Maou's facial reaction, it was a bitter pill to swallow. That, after all, was the central point of most of his and Ashiya's arguing last night. Even in a place like Villa Rosa whose motto was essentially total freedom—no deposit, no key money, no maintenance fees, essentially no building-upgrade fees, a landlord who was never on premises—the rental contract said "no pets," just like a lot of shared apartment buildings.

In cases like these, exactly what "no pets" means is often up to the discretion of the landlord. Sometimes they would allow animals like small birds or fish. But with anything whose noise or smell would bother other tenants, or otherwise affected the condition of the building—it was a given that those were off-limits. It wasn't exactly a deep, dark secret that cats love sharpening their claws on whatever's handy, either.

"But you don't have any idea where your landlord is right now, do you? You could probably get away with it for a little while."

The rather non-Heroic insinuation from Emi was greeted with Maou bitterly turning toward the plastic-covered hole in the wall. "Yeah," he said, "but thanks to *that*, the property management guy's been here a few times."

"Oh..."

Right. That, Emi thought. Half-wrecking your apartment probably *would* get management involved, wouldn't it? In fact, quite a lot about the demons' current housing situation relied completely on the good graces of their mysterious landlord. A breach of contract wouldn't be the best way to remain in said graces.

"That, and there's *that* problem."

"What problem?"

Maou pointed at the Devil's Castle closet. Emi and Suzuno realized that Urushihara, seated on the floor just a moment ago, was gone.

"Indeed," Ashiya caustically moaned. "We already have one loud freeloader eating us out of house and home. With this in the household, he will be several times louder still."

"...*ksh*," came the muffled sneeze from behind the closet door.

"I guess Urushihara's allergic to cats or something."

"What?!"

The thought never occurred to Emi, despite the near-comical

amounts of sniffling. "Demons can have allergies?" Emi asked, honestly curious.

"Of course they can," Suzuno countered. "We did not call it as such in the Church hospitals, but the study of epidemiology is well on its way within our confines. People in Ente Isla have even died from anaphylactic shock brought about by a bee sting."

"Huh. Maybe we should keep a cat on hand for the *next* time Lucifer hatches some kind of diabolical plan."

"Dude, no!" came the closet-based protest. "This really sucks, okay?"

Emi, instead of replying, tried pushing the box toward the closet, slowly so as to keep from startling the kitten. Maou gently stopped her.

"So basically, we can't keep him here, but it's not like our landlord's a monster or anything. If we say we're keeping him here until we find an owner, I'm pretty sure she's not gonna say no to that, you know?"

"Dude, instead of currying favor with a landlord who isn't here, think about the health of someone who *is* here, okay? *Koff koff...*"

Maou ignored the voice from the closet.

"So, yeah—do you know anyone interested in adopting that guy?"

"...Who would *I* know?" Suzuno indignantly replied. Maou then turned his expectant eyes to Emi, who kept her eyebrows low and tensed.

"I'm pretty sure you know this, but I can't have pets in my building, either."

She was referring to her own apartment in Eifukucho, three train stops away from Maou's home base in Sasazuka.

"Yeah, I know, but you're a call-center lady, right? You think anyone in your office is in the market?"

"I wouldn't get my hopes up," Emi said, "and before that, I'm the Hero, all right? Not just a 'call-center lady.'"

"Yeah, yeah, yeah," Maou said with a sigh. "Guess I'll ask around my work, then."

"He doesn't look that young, though," a dejected Emi observed.

"Especially with that full coat of silver fur and everything. Who'd dump him on the street at *this* point?"

"Yeah, no kidding," Maou nodded. "Like, he was shivering all by himself out by the garbage bins. I felt kinda…bad about it."

"You *what?*" Emi shot back.

"Uh, never mind. So," Maou anxiously said, attempting to bounce the conversation off Suzuno instead, "I guess you're gonna get some more noise from your neighbors for a bit, but I promise it's temporary, all right?"

"Hmph. You were hardly ever quiet neighbors in the first place."

"Lemme pet Meow Meow!"

Alas Ramus could wait no longer. Her legs began to flail in the air.

"Hey, let her pet the guy a little bit."

"Oh, all right," Emi droned. "She's probably gonna be clinging to him all day, you realize."

Then she released Alas Ramus, both her and Maou keeping a close eye on her to prevent too much stimulation for either party.

"…Do *not* say anything," Ashiya told Suzuno as they watched the trio.

"I am not. I was just marveling at what a nice, tranquil family they have become."

"I *told* you not to say anything."

✳

The next day:

"It was abandoned out back? Oh, that's terrible!"

Chiho Sasaki, Maou's shift coworker at the MgRonald in front of Hatagaya rail station they both worked part-time at, sounded legitimately resentful as he walked with her, pushing his bicycle along on one side. As the only person in Japan who knew about Maou, Ente Isla, and why Emi had so many hang-ups about him, she was accompanying the Devil King on the way to his castle.

Getting to play with a kitten was always fun, yes…but there was something else she was trying to bring across to him.

"Yeah, I was pretty freaked out, too." Maou sighed. "It never really comes when you expect it, y'know? I dunno if me picking him up was the right thing or not, but it's gotta beat being under the grease bin, at least."

"Ha-ha-ha…"

Maou let out an even deeper sigh when they reached the apartment building. Chiho, for her part, smiled blankly as she looked up at the frail sheet of hard plastic bravely attempting to cover up the cavernous hole in the wall.

The gloom continued on the way up the stairs and through the door.

"Yo, I'm back—huh?"

Quite outside his expectations, the room was completely quiet. Maou swiveled his head around for an explanation.

"Oh, is nobody here?" Chiho asked from behind his shoulder.

"…Ashiya's oud shobbing," said a voice out of nowhere.

"Agh!"

Chiho leaped into the air in surprise, not expecting Urushihara in the closet.

"Shopping? What about the cat?"

"I'unno. He wuz dalkin'uh Bell 'boud id, tho."

"Um, do you have a cold, Urushihara?"

Before the nasal voice could answer, Ashiya arrived at the door, shopping bag in hand.

"Ah, Your Demonic Highness…and Ms. Sasaki as well."

"Hello, Ashiya!"

"Are you here to look at the kitten?"

Chiho nodded. "Yeah, I thought maybe somebody at school would want it, so…"

"Oh! Well, superb, then… I apologize, my liege. There were a few items I needed to pick up, so I left the kitten under Bell's watch."

"Oh, was that it?"

It was the logical choice. Urushihara didn't want to go near the thing, but the kitten was still young enough that he could no doubt find hundreds of ways to maim himself while Ashiya was gone.

"Well, here, let's get 'im back. We're borrowing her kitchen already—I don't wanna owe her even more."

"Yes, my liege." Ashiya placed the bag on the center table, then knocked on the door to Room 202. "Bell, it's me. We are ready for the cat now."

"…?"

A few moments passed. No response.

"Where is she?"

"Perhaps Suzuno took a nap."

"It couldn't have been more than half an hour, though… Hmm?"

Then Ashiya noticed that Suzuno had absentmindedly left the door unlocked. Not that he cared about the cleric's safety. The cat would always take first priority. He gave the door another knock.

"Bell? I'm coming in. Do you have the—"

Once the door was fully open, he stopped.

"……………………………………"

"*Meww, meww, rrrrr…*"

There, before him…

"……………………………………"

"*Rrrrroowwww…*"

…was Suzuno, eyes deadly serious and breathing heavily through her nose as she poked at the cat's stomach and paws.

"Um, Suzuno?"

"……………………………Oh."

It took Chiho's question to stop Suzuno from propping the kitten up and scratching his neck a little. Realizing she and the two demons were there, her face reddened for more reasons than simply the pink and orange of twilight that filled the room.

"Um, I… No! This is not what it looks like! I, I was merely…"

"*Mew?*" protested the cat as Suzuno hurriedly trundled him back into the cardboard box and turned her back to it.

"Suzuno, your sleeves are covered in cat hair."

"Ah, ahhh…"

Maou pointed at one of them. It was, as he said, covered in a fine layer of silvery sheddings.

"N-n-n-no! No, this is just, um…!"

"If you like 'im *that* much, you could've just said so…"

"He is yours, all right?! Take him back!!"

She slammed the door on Maou—but only after ensuring the box was safely in his arms.

"Oooh, look at that little guy!"

The gasp was audible in Chiho's voice as she sized up the silver kitten snuffling around in his box.

"When you said silver, you weren't kidding, huh? That's pretty striking!"

Maou had spent his previous shift at MgRonald asking around the staff on hand to see if anyone had a feline-shaped hole in their hearts that needed filling. He doubted anyone would bite immediately, and as he feared, both Chiho and Kisaki, his manager, hemmed and hawed at the idea, as did everyone else. Most everyone working at the Hatagaya location lived alone in cheap, pet-free rented apartments as well.

"Boy, it's too bad my dad's allergic," Chiho lamented as she peered into the box. Chiho's family actually owned their place, for a change, and they didn't have any pets a cat wouldn't work with. But, she claimed, her father, Sen'ichi Sasaki, was just as allergic to them as Urushihara.

"You don't know anything about who could've owned him before?"

"Nah. Hell, even if I did, I'm not about to return him to someone willing to abandon a kitten on the street."

"Yeah, good point. Ooh, he sure is cute, though…"

Chiho couldn't wipe the smile off her face if she tried. Especially now, in the light of the sunset making its way into Devil's Castle, reflecting gold off the kitten's silver fur.

"Hmm?"

It was then that Ashiya, in the kitchen, heard a knock at the door.

"Alciel?" Suzuno's hesitant voice mumbled.

"What is it, you crazy cat lady?" the uncharacteristically sarcastic Ashiya replied.

"...Emilia and Alas Ramus are here."

"...One second."

Ashiya winced to himself as he unlocked the door. He was a demon, a proud one at that, and now it had all but become the norm for him to entertain Heroes and Church clerics in his own home.

"Meow Meow!"

There he found Emi, still in what looked to be her work uniform, and Alas Ramus, not-so-obediently staying in her arms.

"She really loves that guy," Emi explained listlessly as she came in. "All day at work, it was just 'meow meow meow meow' the whole time..."

"Yeah? Well, keep her on her best behavior, okay? He's sleeping right now."

It was a perfectly normal conversation between a pair of perfectly normal parents. Too bad there was nothing normal about it at all.

"*Shhhh*, okay?" Emi warned instead of issuing any protest at Maou. Alas Ramus responded by putting her index finger to her own lips, imitating her mommy. Then she added the middle finger for effect.

"Meow Meow's sleeping, all right? We can watch him, but we'll have to be quiet."

"Okey! Shhhh, okay?"

It was questionable how much she understood, but Chiho still surrendered her spot by the box so Alas Ramus could have a closer look.

"Meow Meow sleepy?" the child asked after she peeked inside.

"Mm-hmm," replied Emi, finger back on her lips. "Don't wake him up, all right?"

"Hey, so was anyone at your work interested?" Maou asked.

"Yeah, I asked around, but most of my coworkers are in rentals, so they couldn't take him even if they wanted to. I haven't asked everybody yet, but..."

Emi's career involved working at a customer-service call center for the DokoDemo cell phone provider downtown.

"Oh." Maou shrugged as he looked around the Devil's Castle crowd. "Guess I can't do much keeping this to friends and family, huh?"

"...Who're you calling *friends*?" Emi growled, a bit prickly that Maou counted her in that group.

"Ahh, you know what I mean."

"I wish I didn't."

Emi wanted to continue, but declined, bringing Alas Ramus and the sleeping kitten into consideration. "So...what, then? If you can't find anyone, are you gonna just keep him?"

"I can't," Maou sighed. "That's the whole problem."

Emi sighed a little at the sight of the Devil King so easily brought to the end of his rope. "Well, if 'friends and family' aren't enough, why don't you ask someone else?"

"Oh?"

"You know, the usual way. There're posters like that all over Ente Isla. They usually post them in front of churches or the village mayor's house."

A flash of recognition crossed Maou's face.

"Posters, huh?"

"Indeed, my liege," Ashiya added, showing rare agreement with Emi. "A poster in a conspicuous location may attract the attention of quite a crowd."

"Yeah, I tried making one, actually."

"Agh!"

Emi yelped at the sight of a hand extending out from the closet. She knew it had to be Urushihara, but there was still something classically horror-film about a disembodied hand with a single piece of paper, craning itself out of a closet in an old, beat-up apartment building at dusk.

"L-Lucifer?! Don't scare me like that!"

Urushihara tossed the paper into the air and slid the door shut.

Chiho picked it up. It was a very simple affair—a few lines of word-processor text with a digital-camera photo pasted in.

"Since when did you guys have a camera and a printer?" Emi asked, shooting a glare at Maou.

"Oh, uh, they were both supercheap," Urushihara's voice said. "I figured we should keep Alas Ramus's pics around in as many formats as possible."

"I *hope* you got this old crap supercheap," Maou countered, "or else you got totally ripped off."

Emi, for her part, was more concerned about why, if Devil's Castle had this much discretionary income floating around, they weren't willing to purchase so much as a futon for Alas Ramus during her stays here. She didn't get a chance to verbalize it.

"Umm..."

Chiho apologetically turned to Maou.

"What's this 'Silverfish' thing here?"

Maou took a look at the poster Chiho handed to her. Next to the photo was the line "NAME: Silverfish" in large print.

"Ah," Ashiya boasted, "Urushihara and I thought that up earlier."

"...Uh, could you think a little harder? This is a *cat*, man."

"Well, there is no saying how much longer we may have this kitten," the completely serious Ashiya continued. "We have to be careful handling it, lest the landlord or the management company find out. Call it more of a code name than an actual one."

"Hell of a name," Emi interjected. Considering they were counting on the general public to help with this, the idea of referring to the cat in code words seemed a little noncontributive. But even Maou was starting to have qualms about throwing the word *cat* around the apartment all the time.

"Well, Silverfish or not," he said, "does this look all right to you? We could add another photo or two, put up my phone number, and write 'kitten for adoption' or something on the top..."

The poster itself, while clearly banged up in a few minutes on a home PC, was more than ample for the purpose. Emi disliked the idea of Urushihara taking the initiative here, but there was no point asking for much more. But:

"Where would you put it, though?"

Everyone had a general idea of likely locations. Everyone except Chiho, whose eyes darted between Maou and the poster.

"Where? How 'bout just, like, a telephone pole or something?"

"Yeah, that's what I was thinking," Emi added, failing to see what Chiho's problem was. "That's where you see lost-pet posters and stuff, don't you?"

"Ooh, that's actually not too good of an idea," Chiho diplomatically explained. "For one thing—and I know this is kind of overstating it—but stapling a poster or something on a pole like that is damaging public property. The city of Tokyo's got all kinds of regulations about using telephone poles like that, and I heard the public safety board's kind of serious about enforcement these days..."

"Damaging public property? It's just a pet adoption poster."

Everyone else in the room couldn't hide their surprise.

"Well, sure, if it's just a poster like this, a policeman would probably just tear it down. Maybe give you a verbal warning, at worst. But the way my dad put it, that's not the issue so much as the kinds of trouble you run into if you print your phone number on it."

"Oh...that sort of thing?"

Harmless prank calls were one thing, as Chiho put it, but there had apparently been cases of stalker activity, people posing as the pet's owner to extort the other party, even home invaders who called the number first to ensure no one was home.

"You're the only one with a phone number you can post up, right, Maou? I probably wouldn't do that if I were you. Those creepy door-to-door salesmen might still have their eye on you, for all we know."

"Pardon?" Ashiya asked. "There were some salesmen?"

"...Uh, right! Gotcha! Loud and clear, Chiho! No posters on telephone poles! I sure ain't falling for *that* trick!"

It hadn't been that long ago—not long after Suzuno arrived—that Urushihara fell victim to just such a pushy salesman at their home.

The resulting chaos almost ruined the Devil's Castle finances. They had solved the issue without Ashiya becoming aware of it, and Maou wanted to make damn sure it stayed that way.

"Sorry for raining on your parade after you made this and all, though… You too, Urushihara."

"Ah, it's fine," Maou replied as he folded up the poster and tossed it in the trash bin. "Besides, Chi, you're right. It's my associate here's fault for wanting to post my number all over the place."

"Aw, dude, I got all these pet forums open and stuff, too… Agh!"

Maou kicked the closet door before Urushihara could continue.

"Yeah," Emi said, "I guess this isn't like the kind of countryside I grew up in. It's been nothing but good people around me ever since I showed up here, so I kinda forgot about that. There's no telling who you'll run into, really."

"Emilia?"

Suzuno gave her a surprised look.

"Hmm? What?"

"…No. It is nothing."

The Hero's reply came so naturally that Suzuno was unable to pursue it further.

"So," Emi continued as she lifted up the feline-enthralled Alas Ramus, "I guess we'll have to keep pounding the pavement, huh?"

"Ah! More Meow Meow!"

"You're going home?"

"I got work tomorrow. I'll keep asking around the office, but don't expect any miracles."

"Sure. Um, thanks."

"Well, see you later, Chiho."

"Bye-bye, Meow Meow! Bye-bye!"

"Have a good one, Emi!"

"…Also, Devil King?"

"What?"

Emi glanced at the cat, then Maou. "You know," she said softly, "it's gonna be awful hard to give him up once you feed him for a couple days. You've already given him a name and everything. Don't come crying to me if it winds up becoming a big tearful good-bye tomorrow."

"...Huh?"

"Anyway, see you."

Emi took Alas Ramus and went out the door.

"What was that about?" Maou asked, scratching his neck. Chiho gave him a worried look. Maybe something about it had hit home with her, too.

What it was, although Maou had no way of knowing it, was this: Without any kitten to take care of, and without Maou aware of the fact that Alas Ramus had fused with Emi, what would there be left to keep him here on Earth?

"Try not to get too depressed if someone shows up to adopt him, okay, Maou?"

"Geez, you too, Chi?"

"Mew."

The kitten chose the perfect time to get a word in edgewise.

"Wish someone would clue *me* in on what you're talking about. Huh, Silverfish?"

Silverfish didn't answer.

✳

Three days passed. They tried everything. Emi and Chiho called upon everyone they could think of, but both of them reported no particular leads.

"I asked around the neighborhood, too," Maou lamented. "Now what?" He had gone so far as to call upon Hirose, proprietor at the bike shop where he purchased his beloved Dullahan II fixie, as well as Mr. Watanabe, the elderly local who stopped by MgRonald more days than not for a little something or other. The results were always the same.

If this kept up, they might really have to keep Silverfish hidden from the landlord for God knew how long.

"Mewww..."

Something about Silverfish's meowing sounded despondent to them. Maou took a look inside the box. *Maybe,* he found himself thinking, *I should've just taken him back where I found him. Like Ashiya told me to.*

One of his roommates was allergic, after all—though he had no way of knowing that beforehand—and he wasn't allowed to keep pets in here anyway.

Given Silverfish's unusual coloring, Maou had figured anyone actually capable of keeping cats would've taken him home in a heartbeat.

Then again, though, it was really cold that night. He had found him in the wee hours, with few people around, meowing weakly. To Maou's eyes, he sounded ready to die at any moment. Even he knew it was downright weird of him to be concerned about the fate of a single abandoned kitten, given his post as Lord of All Demons and everything. If it were Ashiya or Urushihara there by that grease bin, they wouldn't have given him a second glance. And Maou wouldn't have blamed them.

Still:

"Guess I'm getting soft... Thinking I oughta come up to you just because of that."

He couldn't help but see a bit of himself in Silverfish. His younger self, clad in rags, thrown to the ground, simply waiting for death to come along.

"Your Demonic Highness? Did you say something?"

Ashiya, fresh from making some warm milk for Silverfish over in Suzuno's room, chose that moment to come back. Maou shook his head.

The Great Demon General was used to the milk process by this point. He picked up Silverfish by the scruff. He responded by naturally opening his mouth.

"It is your meal time, Silverfish," Ashiya said as he brought the feeding syringe to his mouth. But...

"...Silverfish?"

"What? What is it?"

Ashiya sounded annoyed about something. "It doesn't seem to want to drink, my liege... Come on, Silverfish, do you want it to get—"

"Whoa! Ashiya!" Maou, noticing their pet was not his normal self, grabbed Ashiya by the shoulder. "Ain't he shivering?"

"You...you are right. Best to return it to the box, then."

He did. Silverfish responded by taking two or three unsteady steps, then cowering to the ground, bereft of strength.

"*Meww...*"

"Silverfish!"

"Geh," Maou groaned.

Still in his crouched position, Silverfish then relieved himself. It was watery, nothing like the solid performance from yesterday.

"That...that's not good, is it, Ashiya?!"

"Diarrhea, perhaps? I am fairly sure I gave the milk to him at a suitably warm temperature..."

"...*Raoww.*"

"Gahh!!"

Now both of them were in a panic. Silverfish had just spat a glob of something or other out of his mouth.

"Wh-wh-what the hell? He threw up?!"

"I, I swear to you that I did not give it anything inappropriate, my liege!"

The diarrhea was one thing. Now he was throwing up...something.

"Wha-what should we do?! Was I too late or something?! Did he, like, get the flu on the night I found him?!"

Neither Maou nor Ashiya, seeing Silverfish in this sorry state, had any idea what to do.

"Ahhhh-*choo*!!"

"Aghh!!"

The sudden sneeze from the closet sent both of them flying into the air. The closet door was a crack open.

"U-Urushihara?!"

"Stop scaring us like that!"

"Ngh, *duuude*," came the stuffed-up reply as he ran another printout through the slit of the door. "Don't juzt go into a banig or nuffin'. Call a bro."

"A bro?"

"A p-p-*pro*," Urushihara clarified as he flung the paper out and slammed the door shut. Maou picked it up.

"…The Aurora Animal Clinic?"

It was a map to the nearest veterinarian.

✳

"Okay, we'll give your kitty a quick examination, so sit tight, okay?"

Maou gave Silverfish's box to the nurse at the front desk and sat on the waiting room bench, fatigue written deeply around his eyes. He had never been anywhere near a vet's office before, but looking at Urushihara's map, there were actually quite a few of them right near Devil's Castle. He called one of them, explained the symptoms, and they agreed to see him immediately. With extreme care, Maou fastened Silverfish's box to Dullahan II and pedaled off to the Aurora Animal Clinic.

From what he could see in the waiting room, the clinic dealt in all kinds of animals. Cats, of course, but also dogs, birds, even a chameleon, of all things. The room was done up in warm pastel colors, which made it feel different from a hospital, and pet magazines lined the shelves for visitors.

Maou picked one about cats at random, but he couldn't get himself to focus on any of the articles. He took a look toward the examination room door, but nothing was visible from the waiting room. Instead, he spotted a bulletin board with reminders about rabies shots, notices about new medications, and advertisements for the latest and greatest in pet products. It was a world unlike any Maou had interacted with before.

But what struck his interest the most was a photo of a certain dog.

"'Forever Homes Found'…?"

It was a little celebratory piece about all the homes a recent litter of puppies was adopted by. The photo showed a large-breed dog nursing several puppies, a little stick-it note with "ADOPTED!" on it by the head of each one. Maou studied it intently.

"Mr. Maou? We're all ready!" said a short, well-fed man in glasses as he leaned out from the exam room. Maou looked up and tore through the door.

"Silverfish! …Huh?"

There he saw his cat on an examination table, the perfect picture of health, munching on some pet food.

"Huhhh?"

"Yep. I'd say he's perfectly fine."

It hadn't been twenty minutes since he was taken into the room, but Silverfish was now fully walking and eating by himself.

The man, wearing a name plate that read YOSHIMURA: VETERI-NARIAN on it, waved at Maou. "You can have a seat if you like. I'd still say you made the right move bringing him here, though."

"Oh…?"

"Not to get too nosy," Dr. Yoshimura said as he looked at the cat's medical chart in his hand, "but this cat, umm…"

"Silverfish."

"*Silll*-verfish. Um, were you raising this cat in your own home, Mr. Maou?"

"Hmm?"

"Did you get him from someone, or did you find him out on the street, maybe?"

Maou's eyebrows arched upward at Dr. Yoshimura's clairvoyance.

"H-how did you know?"

Instead of answering the question, the vet scrutinized Silverfish's chart. "I think you said on the phone that you were giving him kitten formula…but was there anything else? Like, some of the flakey kitten food he's eating right now?"

"No… He still looked pretty small, so."

"Ah, that's probably why he wasn't feeling too well. It looks to me like Silverfish is old enough that he'll need to start eating solid food. That happens at around the two-month mark, usually. Most adopters would know that, but since you didn't, I thought maybe this was a street rescue of some sort…"

Huh, Maou thought. *It's that obvious to pet owners?*

"He probably got sick because the milk wasn't giving him all the nutrients he needed," Dr. Yoshimura continued. "To put it another way, his diet was so watery that it upset his stomach and gave him that diarrhea."

"Oh…I see," Maou said as he stared blankly at Silverfish's ongoing feast.

"That silver coat of his is pretty uncommon, but judging by those green eyes, it's likely Silverfish is a Russian Blue. Cats in this breed are usually pretty wary of people until they get used to them. He was probably with his mother up to now, but if he got abandoned after that, I'd imagine he's still finding his new environment a little stressful as well."

"Cats can get stressed out…?" Maou had trouble imagining it, but Dr. Yoshimura didn't look like he was joking.

"Oh, it's more likely than you think! Stress can cause stomach ulcers in people, too. Besides, for an immature animal that's gone through a lot of environment changes and maybe without food for a while, it can happen pretty quickly."

Silverfish edged away from the dish, apparently satiated, and began grooming himself.

"By the way, the mass he threw up was a hairball. It's made up of the hair he swallowed while grooming himself like that."

"A hairball?!"

"Yes. Adults usually spit up two or three hairballs a week, on the average. It's totally normal for a cat to do."

"…"

Maou was starting to keenly realize exactly how little he knew about the cats of planet Earth. Silverfish, for his part, was starting to wonder what lay beyond the examination table, so Yoshimura used his practiced hands to place him back in the box Maou provided, keeping them on the lid to keep the suddenly healthy cat from bounding out the top.

"…I never realized he was so healthy," the dejected Maou said. "I think he got a little better once I brought him home, but he never jumped around like *that*."

"Oh? Was he that weak?"

Prodded by Dr. Yoshimura, Maou went ahead and summarized the events of the past few days to him, as they related to Silverfish.

"I guess this was kind of irresponsible of me, wasn't it?"

The vet gave Maou a puzzled look.

"I mean, picking him up even though I was in no shape to care for him. And then he was like *that*, you know? I'd be pretty hopeless if I wound up making him starve to death…"

Ever since he first planted his flag in the ground in the demon realms, Maou always held the philosophy that anyone who joined his force would be fairly treated and generously taken care of. But, without his demonic force, he couldn't even take care of a domesticated animal off the street correctly. He hadn't felt this powerless in at least a century or so.

"Mr. Maou," Dr. Yoshimura replied as he watched Silverfish paw at the walls and chew on the towel inside the box, "you haven't done anything irresponsible at all. I mean, maybe your landlord won't be too impressed…but you're feeding him, you're trying to find a home for him, and you brought him here when you realized something was wrong. If you hadn't picked him up, he might've died before you could even name him, much less have me look at him. You don't have a single thing to regret, I don't think. If anyone's acting irresponsible here, it's definitely the person who abandoned Silverfish in the first place."

Receiving this mental encouragement from a human veterinarian made Maou feel even more hopeless than before. "Yeah," he protested, "but I still haven't found anyone to take him in…"

There was no way he could dump Silverfish on the road now. But after tapping all the (rather meager) social resources he had, nobody stepped up.

Dr. Yoshimura thought for a minute. "Mr. Maou," he began, "did you notice the bulletin board in the waiting room?"

"Oh, about the rabies shots and stuff? ...Oh!"

Along with all those medical notices, he recalled, there was a piece celebrating that recent puppy adoption blitz.

"I can't guarantee we'd find anyone immediately, but would you like to maybe put up a notice on that board? I think Silverfish's got a lot of attractive features, and you don't see a silver cat *this* pretty too often at all. I'm willing to bet one of our regular visitors would love to take a look at him. You'll have to keep him in your home for a little while longer—we don't have a boarding service here, I'm afraid—but I can promise you that we'll refer any qualified candidates over to you."

"Mewww!!"

Silverfish accepted the unexpected offer before Maou could even nod.

"Hmm," Ashiya mused as he looked through his paperwork. "So *this* is no longer considered a child?"

It took something of a dedicated effort to get Silverfish home safe without him clawing the box to shreds in the process.

"They're fully grown after a year, is what he told me. I thought I was gonna need a new box on the way home!"

Even as they spoke, Silverfish was playfully bounding across the tatami mats that lined their room. It was doubtful a cardboard box could do much to confine him any longer.

"All right. So..."

Ashiya warily eyed the other merchandise Maou brought home with Silverfish.

"He said I'd need this stuff as a bare minimum."

Lined up next to Silverfish's box was a package of milk additive for cats, the solid flake-style weaning food the Aurora Animal Clinic recommended to him, a dish to place it in, some kitty litter, a beginner's handbook to raising kittens, and so on.

"It didn't cost as much as it looks," Maou explained. "Even with the admission fee, it was only around seven thousand yen."

Ashiya's face tightened at the lofty figure, but:

"Meww! Mewww!"

His eyes met Silverfish's round, beady ones as he sidled up to him, padding elegantly across the room, then stopping occasionally to look up at the ceiling.

"Well," he observed, "perhaps it is all for the best."

"Pssht! ...Meww."

"Heh, um, ummm, *so*, how much of this weaning food should I give him per meal...?" Ashiya asked.

It was the sensation of Silverfish's fur against his leg that caused Ashiya to make that sequence of odd noises near the beginning of his question. He walked carefully to avoid stepping on him, but Silverfish remained constantly at his feet, refusing to retreat. The sight forced Maou to crack a smile, but then he went to his shopping bag again, remembering something.

"Also, I went to the pharmacy and brought a pretty good-looking allergy mask. Make do with this for a little while, Urushihara."

"Come *onnnnn*, dude!!"

"Meww! Meww! Meww!"

The fallen angel's complaint from the closet was half screamed. Silverfish left Ashiya's feet and meowed at the door, as if teasing him.

"It is utter chaos in there," Suzuno remarked over in the other room—but if anything, her voice betrayed her relief that Silverfish was fine after all.

More time passed.

Silverfish, now fully used to the Devil's Castle cast of characters, had regained his kitten-like playfulness, distracting the demons from their world-domination plans on a regular basis. Still, this *was* the Devil King and the best of his four top generals. They never deviated from Silverfish's prescribed feeding plan, and they took steps to keep him from bashing into furniture during particularly heated play sessions. It was to the point that they could instinctively sense his potty breaks before he took them on the litter.

Ever resourceful, the demons even took pains to replace the

threadbare towels they placed in Silverfish's box for extra comfort. The feline milk they purchased for emergency purposes was just about to run out. The jingly cat toy Maou bought at the hundred-yen shop was already a favorite of its target, to the point that Silverfish would thrash around on it without Maou having to wave it around for him.

"...You seriously think you'll be fine if an adopter shows up?"

"Do not bother asking me."

"Aw, he's so cute!"

Emi, Suzuno, and Chiho could only watch as the two grown demons messed around with the silvery ball of fur.

"Ahh-*choo*!!"

Urushihara also provided his own commentary.

A few more days passed. It was now nearly two weeks since Silverfish had entered their lives.

"...!"

Maou's phone received a call from the Aurora Animal Clinic. It was right in the middle of his now customary evening kitty playtime, and it almost made him break out in a cold sweat.

"Hi, Mr. Maou! This is Dr. Yoshimura. We had someone in here today who's interested in adopting Silverfish."

"Oh...really?"

"Mewww? Meww! Meww!"

Silverfish, miffed at the sudden lack of play, started climbing up Maou to get his attention. Maou tried to shake him off as he kept up the phone conversation before he ripped up his shirt. Ashiya, looking on, was already feeling a wistful sense of passing in his brain. Urushihara held his breath...and sneezed.

"..."

By the time phone conversation ended, Silverfish was on Maou's shoulder, forgetting his initial objective and trying frantically to scale his master to the very top.

"We got an adopter."

"...So we do, my liege."

"The vet told me it's a good one. He's got a lot of experience with cats and stuff, and he said his last one lived a lot longer than average."

"...Well, what more could we ask for?"

It was cause for celebration, but both Maou's and Ashiya's voices were gloomy and restrained.

"It sounds like we can take him in tomorrow. We're free to say no, of course, but..."

"...I doubt we have any right to, my liege. The cat, sadly, has no right to be here."

The whole reason for the adopter search was because Silverfish couldn't spend his life in this room. Now he had the ideal owner. They had no reason to refuse.

Maou picked up Silverfish, who had just completed his epic journey to the top of his head, and brought him close to his face.

"Great news, huh, Silverfish? You've got a new master."

Looking down at his oddly sullen temporary master, the young Silverfish opened his mouth wide, as if to yawn.

"*Roww...pfft.*"

"...Could you cough up a hairball some other time, please?"

This was nowhere near as emotional a moment for Silverfish, as evidenced by the current frenzied flailing of all his legs.

"We better let Emi and Chi know, too. They helped us out a lot with him. Tell 'em they don't have to worry about us eating him from now on, huh?"

By now, of course, it was far too late to go back. Maou and Ashiya both had developed a special, unique affinity for the kitten.

"Meow Meow go to the doctor?"

Alas Ramus looked up from the child seat installed on Dullahan II.

"Yeah," Maou nodded as he pushed the bike with him. "We're gonna go meet his new owner."

Inside the box fastened to the front was Silverfish. It had been his first time out in a while, and that had put a dent on his usual frenzied playfulness.

Emi, for whatever reason, had decided to show up with Alas

Ramus after he gave her the news. She asked how far the vet's office was, and after confirming it wasn't a long distance, took the almost unheard-of step of letting Maou take the child over there. "She won't have a chance like this again, after all," she rationalized.

"Have you caught the kitty flu or something?" said Maou, a bit stunned by the non-Emi-like offer.

"Well, I got to talking with Rika about it," Emi replied with the casual, low-tension manner she had exhibited a lot of lately. "She said that when you give an animal up and you're alone, it feels totally awful on the way back. Hey, why don't you go out to eat somewhere with her, too? It's still hot, though, so make sure she doesn't get dehydrated."

"...You're creeping me out even more now."

Not only did Emi figure out how broken up he was over Silverfish's departure, she was virtually giving him a consolation gift.

"Oh," she chided, "so you'd prefer if one of us watched you bawl your eyes out after you give the cat up?"

Maou had little answer to that.

"If you wanna go by yourself, then fine," she continued. "Did you hear that, Alas Ramus? Daddy doesn't want to be seen with you in public anymore. What do you think about—"

"All right! I'll take her!!"

Brushing off the ever-malicious Emi, Maou pedaled off to the Aurora Animal Clinic, Ashiya, Suzuno, and Chiho seeing him off with eyes full of regret.

Alas Ramus swung her arms in the air as she walked, singing a bizarre melody of "Meow meow, meow meowwww" in no particular key. Maou smiled at her and walked on, trying to keep the box steady as he slowly walked to the clinic, savoring the moment.

He parked his bike by the building's wall, removed Alas Ramus from her seat, then—with a word of warning to keep calm—unfastened the rope keeping Silverfish's box in place. Alas Ramus toddled along beside him, holding both hands against her face for some reason.

"Why're you covering your mouth, Alas Ramus?" a curious Maou asked.

"I'm a good girl. Ssshh!"

In her mind, being a good girl apparently meant shutting up. Maou smiled at the effort, although her interpretation of those rules were still a tad childish. It made him feel at least a bit relieved as he opened the door to the clinic.

"Oh, hello there, Mr.... Oh, is that your child, Mr. Maou?"

Yoshimura the vet was already in the waiting room, eyes wide and round upon noticing Alas Ramus.

"Yeah, she's my daughter, pretty much."

"Oh, really?"

"Woof woof!"

Alas Ramus's "sssh" dissipated rapidly at the sight of a large ceramic dog perched by the waiting room entrance.

"Whoa, Alas Ramus! We're in 'shhh' mode, remember?"

"Shhh? Woof Woof *shhh*, too!"

The ceramic retriever was too busy holding an OPEN sign in its mouth to respond. Alas Ramus placed a finger over her mouth at it anyway.

"So who's going to adopt Silverfish?" Maou asked.

"Oh, let me introduce you. Right this way..." Dr. Yoshimura pointed at someone sitting on the bench. He stood up and made Maou's heart skip a beat.

"Whoa! Mr. Hirose?!"

"Oh," exclaimed the surprised Yoshimura, "do you two know each other?"

It was Mr. Hirose, all right—proprietor of the bicycle shop Maou frequented. He had already turned down Maou's kitten offer once, making his presence all the more of a surprise for him.

"Hey, uh, sorry I disappointed you last time, Maou!" Hirose grinned nervously. "Didja hear from Dr. Yoshimura that I used to have a cat at home?"

"Yeah, and...uh, it lived for a really long time?"

"Uh-huh! Pretty much! Used to, anyway. She passed away two years ago."

"I'm sure Luna lived a very happy life with you, Mr. Hirose," Yoshimura gently added.

"Oh, her name was Luna?"

"Ehh, more or less," the ever-workmanlike Hirose confessed. "I had her since back before I got married, so she was actually older than my first kid. The whole family pretty much lost it when she died, I tell you. So I turned you down at first 'cause I didn't think we had it in us to keep a cat besides Luna, but… Hey, you mind if I open the box?"

His hand made for the lid once Maou nodded his approval.

"Meww?"

Silverfish, as if waiting for his cue, meowed with gusto.

"Y'know, I didn't realize it until I saw the pics, but this guy looks exactly like Luna did. She was a Russian Blue, too, and you wouldn't believe how bright and silvery her hair was. I don't think she was pure-bred or nothin', but still, she was a sight to see, y'know? It's almost the anniversary of Luna's death, so I figured I'd call on Dr. Yoshimura and see how things are going, but then I saw your poster, and it felt kinda like…I dunno, destiny or something. What's his name, anyway?"

"Silverfish."

"Silver…?"

The initial confusion quickly gave way to a broad smile.

"Well, you mind if I take him? It's not like I'm aimin' to replace Luna or whatever—I just figure it's about time we add a little one to our family again. I dunno what the kids'll think of '*Sil*-verfish,' but I'll try to get 'em on my side."

"Ah, you can call him whatever you want, sir. Just take good care of him for me, okay?" Maou replied, smiling as he handed Hirose the box.

"Oh, can I go and visit him now and then?"

"Well, of course!"

"Meww."

Silverfish had no objections.

✳

"Oh, he's right here in the neighborhood?"

"Yep! I totally know the guy, too."

"Woof Woof! Woof Wooooof!"

Alas Ramus was carrying a small ceramic dog in her hand.

Emi frowned at Maou, figuring he was spoiling her yet again. "Well, that's too bad," she observed. "I was hoping you'd come back here as brutally depressed as you were when Alas Ramus went away."

"…Thanks a lot."

Maou was more than a bit offput. It sounded like Emi was both razzing him and expressing concern for him at the same time.

"So it was Mr. Hirose? The same Hirose who runs the bike store where all the shops are?"

Chiho had just as clear a grasp of the local geography as Maou had.

"Well, that's great!" she continued. "That's right nearby here! Now you and Silverfish don't have to be lonely at all!"

Somehow, the lack of ulterior motive behind Chiho's encouragement made it feel all the more embarrassing for Maou. "Ahh, it's nothing like that," he countered. "I gotta get all this cat stuff over to Mr. Hirose later on anyway, so it's not like we had some kinda tearful good-bye."

Since they had no more use for the remaining cat paraphernalia laid around Devil's Castle, Maou agreed to give it to Hirose later. They figured having a few familiar toys and such on hand would make the transition easier for Silverfish. The entire kit fit into a pretty small bag by this point. It was only when he put the dangly cat toy inside, fresh bite marks still adorning it, that Maou felt a twinge of heartbreak.

"Y'know, Emi…?"

"What?"

"…Thanks a lot for bringing Alas Ramus over."

"…"

Emi was about to say *See? You're totally depressed after all*, but quickly lost the chance when Maou averted his eyes.

"…It is hard to explain, my liege. It feels like the energy has been sucked out of the room somehow."

That night, Ashiya sighed for what must have been the eight hundredth time.

If anything, Ashiya was experiencing more separation anxiety than his boss. He had shared Silverfish feeding duties with Maou. It would take a while to shake the habit of looking at the clock, then the box in the corner.

Maou, for his part, had made playing with Silverfish a must after every work shift for the past few days. Now he was lying on the tatami mats, nothing to while away the time with.

Urushihara, meanwhile...

"..."

...still hadn't left the closet.

"Look, can you just come out of there already? Silverfish is gone, man. It's gotta be like a sauna in there."

"..."

Maou's pleading made the door open just a sliver. Half of Urushihara's face was visible through it.

"Geez, you don't have to act like a ghost..."

"...Uh, not yet." He shut the door before Maou could respond. "Ashiya, could you *please* vacuum this place for me? Tomorrow's fine."

"Why are *you* ordering *me* to vacuum?" Ashiya sourly replied.

"'Cause it's still there, dude. Silverfish's dander 'n' smell 'n' stuff. It's still making my nose feel all itchy! Please, could you just do it first thing in the...heh...hahhh..."

Urushihara's breathing accelerated in volume for a moment before the big reveal came.

"Hahhhh-*choooo*!!"

"Someone's sure got it rough," Maou remarked. Unlike with Urushihara, there wasn't a trace of Silverfish left on his body.

"Funny to think there used to be a cat in here, huh?" he added.

"Indeed...but, Your Demonic Highness, you are acting like Silverfish has passed away. Let us pray that he enjoys a long and fulfilling life in Mr. Hirose's residence."

"...Yeah." Maou nodded.

"Dude, I'd appreciate it if my sneezing didn't get you all nostalgic for... Behh-*choo*!"

The sneeze made the closet walls shudder, further distressing Suzuno next door.

"Pray for a long and fulfilling life, huh…?"

"My liege?"

"…That might not be such a dumb idea after all."

"Hmm?"

"…Never mind. I'm going to bed. Yo, Urushihara! I'm opening the closet to get a blanket!"

"Whoa! Wait, I don't have the mask on… *Dude*, I told you to wait! Hahh…*choo!*"

While disgusted at the goings-on in Devil's Castle, Suzuno shared one thing in common with the demons: Prayer might be just the thing right now.

"…The Devil King, rescuing a small animal's life…"

The god she was praying to wasn't in the skies above Earth, but she scoped out the stars above her regardless.

"If that virtue can establish even the tiniest of footholds in the Devil King's mind, who can say what will build from there…?"

The summer night rolled on, bringing the heat and the bustle of the city with it—not caring about the thoughts of anyone human or demon below it.

"Hey, Bell, I'm sorry, but could you watch Alas Ramus for me?"

"Ah, Emilia. What brings you here?"

It was evening, the summer sun just beginning to release its grasp on the world, and Emi—presumably fresh from a visit next door—had just interrupted Suzuno's important business of leafing through a kimono catalog.

"Suzu-Sis!" the child exclaimed as she allowed herself to be transferred from one pair of arms to the other.

"I'll be right back, okay?" Emi said before hurrying off, not bothering to give the suspicious woman the reason for the favor.

"Suzu-Sis, that a picture book?"

"...Hmm?" replied Suzuno. "Ah, yes. Well, it *is* a book, yes; one with all kinds of pictures of Japanese clothing, and—"

"I refuse!!" came the thundering interruption through the wafer-thin wall.

"Hmm?" replied Suzuno as she came to her feet, Alas Ramus eyeing her curiously. This was followed by what sounded like an enormous mouse scurrying about on the other side, where the neighbor's closet would be, and then silence.

"...Alas Ramus?"

"Yes, Suzu-Sis!" the girl politely replied, hand in the air.

That shout undoubtedly came from Emi. Emi, who was in the room next to Suzuno's—Devil's Castle, conveniently located in Room 201 of Villa Rosa Sasazuka, which was a cramped, creaky apartment building smack-dab in Tokyo's Shibuya ward. And if Emi Yusa (aka the Hero Emilia Justina over on another world) was shouting inside there:

"Alas Ramus, are…Mommy and Daddy fighting again?" Suzuno asked.

That was the only logical explanation. Sadao Maou, the Devil King Satan on the same other world, was the "Daddy" in that observation, and he must've done something yet again to attract "Mommy's" ire. But, to Suzuno's surprise, Alas Ramus shook her head.

"Uh-uh! Today, I said, I said I wanna sleepy in Daddy's house, but Mommy said go play with you, so…"

"…Oh."

Suzuno's shoulders fell at the news, expressed with the best vocabulary skills Alas Ramus could muster.

"…Hopefully there won't be a storm at the end of this."

✳

"You—you don't have to be so loud all of a sudden!"

Sadao Maou, the chief breadwinner at Devil's Castle, tried to calm his racing heartbeat as he protested.

"It's not 'all of a sudden,'" Emi said as she stared Maou down with her cruel, heroic eyes in the middle of the sunbaked room. "You should have realized the moment I put Alas Ramus in Suzuno's room that I wasn't about to go along with that. I'm letting you see her once every few days because she demands it of me, all right? But that's as far as I'm willing to go! You will *not* let her stay overnight!"

"Such narrow-mindedness for a Hero," exclaimed the other, taller resident next to Maou—Shirou Ashiya, the Great Demon General, strategic genius, and professional househusband.

"You have no right to complain, Alciel!"

"I have heard it all before by now, Emilia. You believe demons such as ourselves will be detrimental to Alas Ramus's education, yes? And for that shallow, baseless reason, you refuse to let the child stay over?"

The history between the trio said as much. They once formed the two sides of a battle for the very fate of the world of Ente Isla—the King of All Demons and his faithful assistant in one corner, the Hero with the holy sword in the other. Emi, with her unique perspective on the demons and how they behaved, had hardly exercised restraint in giving them her unfettered opinions on their good names before.

"And you still call yourself a decent mother?" Ashiya continued. "What kind of Hero—no, what kind of sensible living creature of any kind—would so cruelly deny a mere child the right to be together with her own father? Regarding Alas Ramus, at the very least, is this really the time to let our past conflicts bubble to the surface?"

This was all complicated by the fact that Alas Ramus —currently under the care of Suzuno Kamazuki, better known in Ente Isla as Church cleric and would-be reformer Crestia Bell —was no ordinary toddler. She was the personification of a Yesod fragment, a seed from the Tree of Sephirot that formed the embryos for worlds themselves in their native dimension. She believed Emi to be her "mommy" and Maou her "daddy," and when she first arrived out of the blue in Japan, she resided in Devil's Castle. Following a couple of battles against Ente Isla's angels for control over both her and Emi's Better Half holy sword, Alas Ramus had fused herself into the sword and, by extension, into Emi's psyche, requiring an unplanned move into the young woman's apartment.

All of this drama resulted in the extremely precarious situation of Emi having to team up with her old nemesis for the sake of this child's future in Japan. It was a sort of silent agreement between the two—for *her*, at least—to try not to dredge up the past too much in public.

That was the point Ashiya was trying to bring up. Emi snorted at him.

"Our past 'conflicts'? Alciel, is that seriously why you think I'm refusing this? I mean, it's not *not* the case, but—"

"Yeah, no duh."

Emi ignored Maou's jab.

"—but even if I didn't see you guys as horrible demons, there's no possible way I would *ever* allow Alas Ramus to sleep in here!"

To prove her point, she marched up to the closet, put her fingertips to the sliding door, and flung it open.

"Whoa, whoa, whoa!" came the surprised, sniveling response from the second tier of shelving as a small man tumbled out from it. Emi's initial ranting made him retreat inside, and he had had a literal ear to the door ever since. That was the way Urushihara rolled—Hanzou Urushihara, also known as Lucifer, another former Demon General.

"Geez!" he protested, his hands breaking his fall just in time to keep from going headfirst into the tatami-mat floor. "Give me some warning next time, dudette!"

Emi, ignoring his plight, pointed right at the tier he used to be lying on.

"You see what should be here? Futons! Bedding! Something! If you want Alas Ramus to stay here, at least get some of *that*!"

The three demons fell silent. There wasn't much countering that.

Emi, for her part, wasn't deliberately trying to be the bad guy in this argument. Within reason, she wanted to satisfy Alas Ramus's wishes, too. For the first week of her life on Earth, after all, this cramped single room (a studio apartment, if you were willing to be extremely charitable) was the only home the child knew. It might still be now if it weren't for that whole sword-fusion thing, in fact.

But what happened, happened—and the changes to Alas Ramus's living situation had been pretty drastic. Emi's apartment had air-conditioning, for example. For a child not all that far removed from weaning age (or whatever they had up there on that tree she came from), that was key. It didn't seem like Tokyo would end its habit of setting new heat records anytime soon, and while Villa Rosa Sasazuka had been built in another time and offered fairly decent ventilation as a result, simply standing here and staring at her sworn enemy was making beads of sweat run down Emi's forehead.

The second reason: the futon she was just yelling about. For a woman who hadn't grown up in an environment where sleeping on the floor was a norm, Emi still preferred a full-on bed for her own apartment. Even now, she couldn't forget the first time Alas Ramus slept at her place. "Fluffy! Fluffy!" she kept crying out in joy as she slapped at the mattress. Before then, apparently, it was either the tatami-mat floor, or a bath towel placed on top of said floor. Even in Ente Isla, whose culture and economy weren't even a shadow of Japan's, everyone who wasn't dirt-poor had beds of their own. It was impossible for Emi to figure out why Maou, who clearly managed to keep his head above water despite Japan's high prices on everything, couldn't buy a single futon for his only child, or pseudochild, as the case may be.

"I'm not asking for memory foam or a hundred percent goose down or anything, but having a girl her age sleep on the bare floor is just ridiculous, you know that? Her bones are still forming and everything. If you make her sleep like that, it's gonna stunt her growth!"

The mere idea of three demons lined up in a row, sleeping on tatami in this deadly summer weather, was enough to make Emi burst out laughing. They kept themselves and their domain relatively clean, at least, but there weren't exactly any bottles of disinfectant spray lying around, and this tatami-mat floor couldn't have been that clean.

Maou and Ashiya failed to respond to Emi's completely valid complaint. Urushihara was attempting to nonchalantly climb back into the closet before Emi's gaze stopped him, sending him running toward the window.

"…And, you know, I've been wondering this, but why don't you ever buy futons in the first place? It's not like you're *that* poor, are you?"

As long as they weren't too picky about the store they got them from, they could at least assemble a couple full single-size sets for cheap. Around fifteen thousand yen could get them a setup they could easily use for any season.

Emi looked at the empty space in the closet and sighed.

"I have given up on it," Ashiya growled. "As far as I am concerned, that is merely Lucifer's storage space now."

"Dude, I'm not luggage," Urushihara protested. But the words rang true enough to Emi's ears.

"Okay, so the top tier's out," Emi said. "But you could make some space on the bottom, couldn't you? I don't think there's all that much stuff inside those cardboard boxes."

"Emilia, I don't spend all day in there…"

"I don't really wanna say this," a despondent Maou interrupted as he spread his legs out on the floor, "but before I answer that, lemme ask you this, Emi. All the bedding and appliances and other crap you've bought here—what're you gonna do with it if you go back to Ente Isla?"

"Appliances? You mean the ones I use?" Emi turned an eye to the refrigerator and microwave in the Devil's Castle kitchen.

Maou nodded at her.

"Well, I was thinking maybe I could take them back with me. Like, convert their power source to holy magic or something."

"Seriously? It's okay for you to bring advanced stuff like that into another world? Don't you think they'd burn you at the stake for witchcraft or something?"

Emi knew what he was getting at, but shrugged anyway. "Look, I've traveled across every inch of Ente Isla. I've even followed you here to slay you. I don't think anyone's gonna complain if I want a few amenities in my life after that."

"…Quite the lofty aspirations," whispered Ashiya under his breath. All that work on Emi's part, and the consumer products birthed by Earth's scientists were good enough for her the whole time. Crossing entire dimensions just for a chance at a microwave, a fridge? The second-tier prizes you get for guessing the price of a car wrong in a game show? Talk about a cheap date.

"Yeah, I guess I'm not all that different," Maou said. "I'd love to have that microwave back home, too—hell, maybe two or three more fridges, even. Still…" He glanced at the closet looming behind Emi. "Futons…don't exactly work that way. Think about it. We're demons."

"So?"

"Like, Urushihara's one thing—he didn't change much in the transformation. But even now, a blanket's startin' to not be enough for Ashiya, you know? Or for me, for that matter."

Now Emi understood. These demons were in human form—for now. But their actual forms were large, demonic, and all-powerful. Maou and Ashiya in particular, back at home, were far larger than any human being could ever be. Which meant…

"Pfft!"

Emi chuckled to herself, trying to picture the cloven-hoofed demons trying to fit in a futon. Maou, guessing this would happen, winced.

"Well, that's…*ffppfftt*! That's fine, isn't it?" Emi asked. "You'd be a Devil King of the people! Your own futon and everything! Maybe you oughta go for memory foam so that horn I cut off doesn't bother you at night! Bah-ha-ha-ha!"

"Enough laughing!" exclaimed Ashiya, face reddened. "Enough imagining His Demonic Highness in a human futon already!"

"Ashiya, do you have to spell it out like that? *You* imagined it, too. That hurts my feelings a little."

"Gah!"

"…Anyway. Even if we buy futons, we can't use 'em back there. Besides…" Maou crossed his arms and sat back, looking up at Emi. "If we did buy that stuff, that's pretty much declaring to the world that we're just fine shackin' up in this world for good. I just didn't want to buy 'em, okay? Japan, to me at least, is just a rest stop."

"Ahhh…ha-ha-ha-ha…" Emi, finally composing herself again, brought a hand to her hip. "The King of All Demons, playing mind games with himself like that? Puh-leeze. And you better not give that reasoning to Chiho, either."

"…"

Emi bringing up the name of a certain girl absent from the room drove her point home even harder. Chiho Sasaki, high-school teen and the only girl in Japan who knew the whole truth behind Ente Isla and everyone currently in the room, still had feelings for Maou anyway. If she heard him proclaim to the world that he was just doing the equivalent of couch-surfing in this world, it would dishearten her, to say the least. She was a good friend to Emi, for that matter.

"...Well," Maou deflected the subject, "besides, buying a set of three futons is gonna set us back a pretty decent amount, isn't it? We ain't *that* well off yet, so I figure—hey, if we made it this far without 'em, might as well go all the way."

"All right..." Emi wasn't willing to delve into Maou's finances, but something still made no sense to her. "But you've been here in Japan for over a year by now, haven't you? What'd you all do last winter?"

A little urban camping wouldn't hurt them much in the summer, but going without a futon in midwinter Tokyo seemed like suicide to her.

"Oh, that?" Maou pointed at the low table in the center of the room. "When I bought that, it came with this wimpy little *kotatsu* heater inside it. After that, we just put on a bunch of layers, and I had Ashiya sleep opposite to me and we stuck our legs under there."

"Oh my God..."

Maou proudly placed his palm on the dining table/writing desk/ etc. in front of him. Urushihara, still inexperienced with Japanese winters, groaned.

"...Well, I'm not gonna complain if you all freeze to death this winter," Emi said. It really seemed that way to her. These demons were gonna get themselves killed even if she didn't bother slaying them. But that still didn't solve the problem at hand. "So be it. Like you said, Alciel, I care for that girl, so... I'll pay for it."

"Really?!"

"What?!"

"Dudette!!"

Emi glared at the wide-eyed demons, doubting their gratitude.

"*Alas Ramus's*, all right? Why do I have to pay for *yours*? Also, you're her 'daddy,' remember? We're going Dutch on this or nothin'."

The wave of depression this statement generated was as palpable as it was dramatic. Emi wished she had it on video.

"Ugh," groaned Emi to herself on the commuter train the next morning. "Why did I have to go that far?"

She knew it wouldn't be fair to Alas Ramus to shut off visitation rights entirely—that much, she was willing to accept. The problem was the holy-sword connection between "mother" and daughter. It prevented the two of them from being physically separated beyond a certain distance. Which meant, naturally, that Emi would need to be near Devil's Castle if Alas Ramus wanted to sleep in peace in there.

A night in Suzuno's place next door would suffice, although it'd be imposing terribly on her friend. But would Alas Ramus be willing to accept that?

On the night before their first battle with the angel Gabriel and his minions, Emi, Maou, and Alas Ramus spent a single "family" night together at his place. If the child still had vivid memories of that stayover, she'd all but demand a repeat—all three of them together again. Nobody had any futons at the time, so it wasn't like Emi was "sleeping with" Maou (in so many words).

But Emi had even more serious, nonimaginary reasons to be concerned.

"It's not like I could kick out Alciel and Lucifer, either..."

From a purely physical perspective, there was no sleeping space left in Devil's Castle for Emi. Things were different from the last time she stayed over. As small as Urushihara was, three men lying in that tatami-mat space would immediately fill it up. There would be only the barest of gaps for Alas Ramus, just like how it was last time. If Emi was going to somehow snake her way between the computer desk and table to stay near Alas Ramus, that would put her dangerously close to the other demons as she attempted to sleep.

Even if it was for Alas Ramus's sake, certain things were simply off the table for her—as a Hero, and also as a woman.

"Could we store Lucifer in the closet? ...Hmm, maybe not."

Seeing him emerge from the closet, like some kind of ghost possessing the apartment building, would undoubtedly make Alas Ramus burst into tears. Urushihara and Ashiya stayed at Suzuno's place during the last "family" meetup, but that was under extremely exceptional conditions.

"I guess," Emi said in a depressed whisper, "I'll just have to make Alas Ramus deal with it." She wondered why she had to worry about any of this, like a divorced parent wrangling over visitation rights. "I have no idea what makes for a good child futon, either... I should've kept my mouth shut."

She turned on her smartphone to find out. The last time she'd purchased any bedding, it was at a local shop—one that didn't deal in children's stuff at all. (She had double-checked on the way home the previous night.) And it wasn't like online shopping would be ideal, either. This was going to be Alas Ramus's futon. Emi would prefer to buy something the child liked, but since she was going in half with Maou, she'd have to consider the Devil King's financial sensibilities or risk getting chewed out endlessly later on.

What would work?

Emi, by now, had fallen into the habit of asking the people around her if something about Japan was confusing her. So, earlier in the day, she had gone up to Rika Suzuki, a coworker and friend at the DokoDemo call center they both worked at.

"Hey, do you know where you can buy a futon sized for children?"

"Huhh?!"

Rika went wide-eyed. She placed her fork down and left her lunchtime pasta bowl be for the time being. The dramatic response put Emi off guard for a moment.

"Like, where'd *that* come from? That's about the last question I would've expected from you, Emi."

"Yeah, well...um, I told you about the kid Maou had at his place, right?"

It wasn't the first time Emi had discussed Alas Ramus with her. But this time, she had brought up the topic a little too naturally for her own sake.

"Right…?"

"Well, right now she's…………."

At that moment, Emi froze. She had totally screwed this up, but she couldn't take the words back now.

"Right now she's what?" Rika asked. "This is the girl who thought you were her mom, right?"

"Y-yeah, but…so, like, that girl, um…"

…*is living at my place.* Emi rued not thinking about Rika's reaction to *that* bombshell a little before speaking up. She was a good friend to her, but unlike Chiho Sasaki, she didn't know who Emi and Maou really were. She knew *about* Alas Ramus, but not what she *was*, exactly—just a relative of Maou's, is how Emi put it.

"She's come to visit now and then…and, like, she's been staying over sometimes…"

Emi knew the words out of her mouth were terribly strained. But there was no changing the subject now. She had to fess up.

"Come to visit? Like, your place? What's up with that? Are you taking care of that Atlas girl or whatever her name was?"

"Alas Ramus," corrected Emi, even though she knew that wasn't Rika's main issue with this revelation.

"She's related to Maou, isn't she? Why are *you* looking after her? 'Cause that's kind of weird, isn't it?"

Well, yeah. Even Emi knew it was weird. Until just a few days ago, really, there wasn't any connection between her and Alas Ramus— nothing besides the child's completely wrongheaded ideas about her.

"Wait… So I'm not saying this is true or anything, but is this Maou guy taking advantage of that girl's fondness for you and making you look after her?"

Emi paused.

"No, no, nothing like that! He's not pushing me into it or anything…"

"So what, then?! 'Cause depending on what this is, I won't be afraid to give Maou a piece of my mind for you, okay? Like, I could probably hook you up with a lawyer from my dad's company, too!"

This was how Rika always ticked. She was always ready to turn any grievance into a civil lawsuit.

"Hey, hey, calm down, okay? I don't need a lawyer from Kobe quite yet. He's not a deadbeat dad."

Emi had to assuage Rika before she started beating down Maou's door. If she did, after all, it'd be just as much trouble for Emi as it would be for him. Regardless of what Maou thought about it, Emi and Alas Ramus were indivisible at this point.

"So," she began, "you know how it is at that age—it's like they miss their mother a lot and stuff, y'know? And Maou's got nothing but guys living with him, and I guess Suzuno living next door isn't good enough for her, so... And Maou's one thing, but I kinda like the girl, so...you know, she's been welcome at my place at times when we really need to do it. It's all clear with his relatives, too, so..."

"Hmm... Well, weird, is all I can say. But if you're cool with it, then fine, I guess."

"Yeah. She's a big fan of Chiho, too, but we can't really leave her in the hands of a minor, right?"

"Well," said Rika, still sounding unconvinced, "leaving her in the hands of someone who's not even his girlfriend isn't exactly normal, either. But that's what you want a child futon for, huh? You aren't gonna pay for it, are you?"

"Nah, Maou's covering all that."

Covering *half* of it. But saying that would accomplish nothing for her.

Rika pondered over this, fork halfway in her mouth. "So, like, a bedding shop or something? I usually go to Torikawa Sleep Center, but that might be kinda out of his price range, by the looks of things."

"...Torikawa, huh?"

It was one of Japan's oldest continually operating retailers, in business for more than four hundred years. As a brand name in bedding, it was well-nigh unstoppable.

"Yeah," Rika hedged, "that might be going overboard, 'specially considering she's gonna outgrow it pretty quick anyway. Though maybe you could just get him to buy a size too big for her instead, huh? I mean, Alas...Ramus, right? She must be gettin' pretty big by now."

Emi's eyes turned skyward. She didn't recall Rika ever meeting the girl before.

"...Oh, I mean, just based on what you've told me about her, that is!"

It might have been Emi's imagination, but she could have sworn Rika gasped for just a moment before speaking up again.

"But anyway! I know going full brand ain't cheap, but you could probably find a Torikawa futon at a discount kids' place like Hishimatsu for a little less. You gotta go online to get the real deals, but I guess you'd want to be sure the kid likes the thing first, huh?"

"Hishimatsu?"

"You never heard of it? They sell kids' clothing and accessories and stuff."

Emi took out her phone to search for it.

"Oh, I've never seen them in the city itself, though," Rika continued, enjoying the iced coffee that came with her meal. "They're mostly out in the suburbs and bedroom communities... Oh! Hey! Maou lives right near the Keio rail line, right?"

"Huh? Yeah," Emi replied, almost dropping her phone at Rika's suddenly loud voice.

"In that case, why don't you try visiting stops like Seiseki-Sakuragaoka and Minami-Osawa?"

"Why's that?"

Emi knew the names, at least, having idly stared at the Keio rail map during more than one boring train wait. Seiseki-Sakuragaoka was a stop on the special-express line, while she was pretty sure Minami-Osawa was one of the stops on the branch line she had never been anywhere near before. Eifukucho, the main station she used, was on the Keio line—but she took the Inokashira line to work instead, switching at the Meidaimae station three stops from Shinjuku, so she knew little about what lay beyond.

"There's a big outlet mall off Minami-Osawa. They sell all kinds of cheap brand-name stuff there, though I dunno what the scene is as far as futons go. Seiseki has a bunch of Keio-run shops right off the station that're pretty cheap. Fun to browse through, too!"

"Hmm. The suburbs then, maybe?"

Emi began searching the station names on her phone.

☀

"Whoa, Alas Ramus. Take your shoes off first."

"No!"

"No pouting. You're gonna get the seats all dirty."

"Awww..."

Emi grabbed the legs of Alas Ramus, eagerly trying to grab a view out the train window, and attempted to wrest the sandals off her feet. It was proving a difficult task.

"Come on, Alas Ramus," admonished Maou across the aisle. "Listen to your mommy."

"...Aww, okeh." With a nod, the girl let Emi do her work, then kneeled on the seat as she took in the outside scene.

"Ugh, she always listens to *you*," Emi said as she followed her gaze out the window.

"Yeah, because I'm more of an authority figure to her."

"Oh, sure, in your T-shirt, shorts, and sandals, right? That just exudes authority."

"Hey, it's hot today. This is what dads wear on their days off, okay?"

Maou took a look around the train car. Emi joined him.

"Whether they do or not," Emi said, "they don't do it if they're as young as *you* are."

There was no point bickering about this any further. Emi sighed just as the PA system announced their upcoming arrival at Chofu station. It was a Sunday train run on the Keio special-express line bound for Hachiouji, and given the early-afternoon time frame, it was fairly crowded. The three of them had managed to find seating close to each other nonetheless.

Emi had informed him earlier in the weekend that they'd be traveling to some station called Seiseki-Sakuragaoka in order to purchase Alas Ramus's futon. They'd have to switch trains at Meidaimae to catch the express one. Maou was dead set against it at first. Looking at the map, it seemed like it was on the other side of the country to him, and Emi's lecturing about prices and selection all flew over his head.

Then Emi put Alas Ramus on the phone.

"I wanna go out with you, Daddy!"

And before he knew what he was doing, he agreed to it.

But if Alas Ramus was going out, that naturally meant Emi would be joining her. He didn't think about that until after he hung up.

"What's that note you got?" Emi asked. Apart from his wallet and phone, it was all Maou had with him.

"Oh. A shopping list. Ashiya told me to buy this stuff if I found it for cheap."

He extended his arm over Alas Ramus. Emi picked up the note, despite herself, and gave it a quick once-over.

"One bag of onions, some *natto*, dishwasher liquid fillers… Is this really stuff you'd go on a train ride to get at a discount?"

"Yeah, I dunno what he's thinking, either."

Maou grabbed the note off Emi's out-thrust hand, jammed it back in his pocket, then suddenly turned toward Alas Ramus.

"Hey, what're you seeing out there, little girl?"

"Mmm, airplane!"

"Oh? Ooooh, you're right. Wow, it sure is high up, huh?"

"And Magrobad."

"Huh?"

"Magrobad!!"

"What's that?"

Alas Ramus was staring right at him, hopping up and down and pointing.

"Uhh…"

"She's pointing at a MgRonald sign," an exasperated Emi explained.

"Oh, really?"

She had spotted a MgRonald facing the roundabout in front of a passing station.

"Daddy! Magrobad!" she shouted, as if she just discovered a new species of fish or bird.

"Ooh, yeah, you're right."

"She's been wanting to eat there all the time lately," Emi flatly stated, keeping Alas Ramus from spotting her pained look. "I keep telling her she's too much of a baby for it still."

"She has?"

"Yeah. She says it 'smells like Daddy.'"

"…Aw, what a good girl you are, Alas Ramus!"

Maou reached out to rub the girl on the head, quite the opposite reaction to Emi's wincing. But then:

"Oww!"

Alas Ramus, forehead plastered to the window, hit her head against it as a passing train whizzed by at full speed, making the glass rattle. The resulting surprise led to predictable results.

"Nn…nhh…*waaaaaaaaahh!*"

"Ooooh, uh… Yeah, I bet that hurt a little, huh? You okay, Alas Ramus?"

Maou picked her up with the hand he was going to pat her with, trying to ease her out of her crying jag.

"S-sorry, sorry," Emi whispered to the passengers surrounding her. Then:

"Oh, come on!"

She groaned as Maou took the seat directly adjacent to her, Alas Ramus on his lap and the annoyed stares of the general public surrounding them.

"…Whew."

Emi and Maou stepped on to the curved platform of Seiseki-Sakuragaoka station, gave each other a look, and sighed.

"Look, Emi, she waged this epic battle against an archangel without breaking a sweat. Why does hitting her head a little against a glass window make her cry?"

"That...that's what I want to know."

Alas Ramus, upon crying herself out, promptly fell asleep in Maou's arms. Even in the humid air that surrounded them, she showed no signs of waking up.

"Raising a kid's just an endless spring of surprises, isn't it?"

"At least I don't have to worry about losing her in a crowd... Hmm?"

As they spoke to each other, a young couple passed by their side, pushing a stroller that contained a child maybe a little younger than Alas Ramus.

"...You could always do that," Maou suggested.

"Ah, there's too many curbs and stairways I have to traverse in my neighborhood. It'd be too much of a pain, and Alas Ramus would outgrow something that size pretty quick anyway."

"Well, hell, I dunno, we sometimes get customers with kids in strollers that look like they oughta be in kindergarten. Oof!"

Maou adjusted his body to get a better grip on Alas Ramus, who was just about to fall out of his arms.

"Yeah, you do, don't you? But for a child this size, I bet they're gonna be pretty...expensive...?"

Out of nowhere, Emi pictured herself right now. Standing right next to Maou, peering at Alas Ramus's face as she slept, having the most normal of conversations with him. Then she recalled their exchanges on the train itself.

"...Um, hello?"

"...Nnngh!"

She immediately sat herself down on a nearby bench.

"What, you gettin' too hot or something?"

The worst part of it was that Maou looked genuinely concerned. She sized him up with her eyes, bottom to top.

"This is like...like we're a real married couple or something..."

The resentment in her voice sounded like it was bubbling up from the underworld.

"...Uh?" Maou arched an eyebrow, feeling a tad insecure. "Look..."

"What?"

"When a girl says something like that, they're *supposed* to act all awkward and flirty and stuff."

Emi began to feel like the heat really would claim her before long.

"*Is* that how you want me to react?"

"Hell no."

"...I swear I'll kill you...ugghh." She stood up, face still pale against the sun. "Let's make sure that doesn't happen again, all right? Let's just finish this shopping trip and go home. This is driving me totally bonkers."

"As if it's not for me."

But despite all that, Emi and Maou still walked down the rail station stairs together. Alas Ramus was there, after all.

"...If Chiho saw us right now, it'd be a disaster, wouldn't it?"

"How?"

"...Never mind," Emi said.

※

"Oh, what a cute little girl! How old is she, ma'am?"

"..."

"...Uhh, she just turned two a bit ago! Ha-ha-ha..."

They were in the baby department of the Seiseki-Sakuragaoka Shopping Center, just a few steps away from the station turnstile. The question from the well-meaning saleswoman immediately froze Emi on the spot, forcing Maou to provide backup with the most strained smile of his life.

"Will you get it together, please?" he snarled as he grabbed the spaced-out Emi by the shoulder. Alas Ramus was still napping in his other arm.

"Agh!" Emi yelped.

"So how can I help you today?"

"Oh," Maou blurted in place of the still-bleary Emi, "we thought you might have a futon big enough for her to use, so..."

"Ah, perfect! Were you using a crib or baby bed up to now, sir?"

"Oh, she was with her mother," Maou replied, too scared to reveal to a stranger that she was sleeping on bare floors.

"...!"

Emi froze yet again.

"Emi, will you please stop spacing out the moment anyone treats us like a family?!"

"Umm," said the saleswoman.

"Oh, sorry, it's no big deal. She was sleeping in the same futon as her mom, I mean."

"Ah, right...with her mother. So she doesn't fuss very much at night, then?"

"...No, not really. She's pretty quiet, I think." Judging by his limited experience with Alas Ramus, Maou didn't imagine she rolled around too much once she was asleep. "Why do you ask?"

"Oh, well, young infants can often act pretty different once they're taken out of their familiar crib or whatnot. I hear from a lot of young mothers who take the step up from cribs to futons, and they're just amazed at how much they start fidgeting all night!"

"I see..."

"Of course, a lot of families don't use cribs at all, so it all comes down to what works best for you! But if she doesn't move around much when she's sleeping, I think it'd be a good idea to provide her with the best futon you can. I have a few different ones I can show you, if you'll come this way..."

"Sure thing. Hey! Emi!"

"...Oh. Yeah."

Maou had to pull Emi's collar to bring her back to reality.

The shelves they were taken to were lined with large, square plastic bags, each one packed with futon sets whose fabric patterns clearly indicated that children were the intended audience.

"Wow," Maou marveled, "some of these come with teddy bears and stuff?"

"Ah, yes," the saleswoman said, nodding, "we find that the transition's easier for a lot of little ones if they have something firm, something reassuring they can clutch to while they're lying down." She pointed at one particular shrink-wrapped bag. "Now, this is one set from our 29,800-yen series..."

"Twenty-nine...!"

Now it was Maou's turn to freeze in place.

"It includes the futon mattress, a comforter that you can adjust for the different seasons, a pillow, some fitted sheets for everything, a hypoallergenic blanket, and this stuffed animal over here. Everything's included in the set. Over in this other shelf, we have sets with summer and winter comforters, along with different covers for each one, and those go for 35,800 yen."

"Thir-r-r-r..."

"Are the covers machine washable?" asked Emi, regaining consciousness just in the nick of time. Or perhaps Emi's subconscious instinctively kicked her brain back into high gear once it spotted Maou's mouth puckering rhythmically, like a goldfish gasping for air.

"Oh, of course!" the saleswoman eagerly nodded as she looked at Alas Ramus in Maou's arms. "Now, based on what the lucky father said..."

Emi tried her best to hang on to her rapidly fading marbles.

"...your daughter doesn't fidget too much when she sleeps, is that correct?"

"Um, I think she's on the more well-behaved side, yes."

"Indeed, indeed. You'll want to watch to make sure she isn't *too* well-behaved, though. With growing bodies like hers, staying in the same position for too long could increase the burden on her bones and muscles. Sleeping in the same position all night can make even grown-ups feel a little sore in the morning, but with young children, it can affect their growth if it's kept unchecked for too long. That's why, if she's pretty well behaved in bed, I'd recommend materials that are as nonresilient as possible."

"Her growth, huh...?"

Something about the saleswoman's pitch resonated in Emi's mind. She turned to the still-asleep Alas Ramus, then shook Maou's shoulder as she looked at the bedding sets on the top shelf.

"Try not to drop her, would you?"

That was enough to bring him back to Earth. He hurriedly adjusted his two-handed grip on her. "Uh, sure, sure!" he protested. "But, like, all of that makes sense to me, but…thirty-five thousand…?"

"Oh, you were listening, huh? …Can I ask you something real quick?"

"Certainly," the saleswoman replied.

Emi took a shallow breath. "Maybe this is a stupid question, but around what age can she use a children's futon until?"

"Well, to be honest…" The saleswoman gave a friendly chuckle. "A lot of it comes down to how your daughter herself grows, in the end, so it can be a bit hard to predict. If a child moves around a lot in their sleep, some people like to go with a larger futon mattress, even if the comforter's the same size. If you decide to go with this package set, I think you would be good to go until about a hundred centimeters, or around three foot three."

"So it depends, huh…?"

"…Emi?"

Maou nodded at the saleswoman's speech, even though Emi's oddly troubled staring into Alas Ramus's eyes gave him some pause. "…All right," he said, "thanks very much. We're gonna browse around for a bit, but do you have a catalog or something like that we can have?"

"Oh, certainly! Take all the time you'd like. I'll bring a few pamphlets over for you."

The saleswoman smiled as she minced into the back area.

"D-Devil King," Emi blurted out.

"Huh?" Maou turned around—and he knew he wasn't imagining it. Emi looked despondent.

"Do you think Alas Ramus will even grow at all? Like a normal child?"

"…!"

He could tell Emi was talking about more than just Alas Ramus's body maturing into an adult. Her concerns didn't involve the responsibility she now had for her, either. It was just that Alas Ramus had the Hero as her mom, the Devil King as her dad, and neither of them were her real parents.

"How are we supposed to even raise her…?"

To Maou, watching Emi as the smiling saleswoman scurried back with a shopping bag full of pamphlets, the scene was downright surreal.

✳

"Y'know," Maou said as they walked down an aisle in their fourth shopping center of the day, "these prices are kinda extreme. I figured thirty thousand was way too much at the first place, but going from that to just three thousand at the second store was kind of fishy, I thought. You think maybe we could thread the needle and find something at around fifteen thousand or so?"

"That one at three thousand was meant for naptime at the day care center," Emi replied. "It's totally different from a futon set that'd get her through the night. And where's *that* coming from, anyway? I thought you were all about saving money."

Maou snorted in response. "Well, I mean, that first one was so expensive, I dunno what the going rate even *is* any longer. I don't wanna shell out too much, but if it's *too* cheap, I start to get suspicious."

He looked down at his feet.

"Hi, Daddy!"

"…Plus, me 'n' Ashiya 'n' Urushihara are all grown-ups and that's one thing, but I'd like something at least a little nice for Alas Ramus, y'know?"

Emi's eyes were on the ground as well. Alas Ramus was awake from her quick afternoon nap, toddling with all her might as she held hands with both of them.

"There's stairs coming up, Alas Ramus. Hang on to Mommy's hand, okay?"

"Okeh!"

"Huh? Wait…"

Alas Ramus gripped Emi's hand tightly. Emi returned the favor.

"Aaaaaaand up we goooo!"

"Aaaiiiiiieee!"

The couple lifted their "child" up in the air over the stairway, the gleeful Alas Ramus hanging from their clenched hands as she made it safely to the top.

"......!!!"

"Geez, Emi, get used to it already! You've been acting like that all day!"

"Mommy, you okeh? Too hot?"

Maou tried to sound as cheerful as possible, while Emi looked about ready to have a seat again. Even Alas Ramus was starting to get concerned. Emi had nobody left to turn to.

"Okay, Mommy looks like she needs a break, so how 'bout we grab some lunch, Alas Ramus?"

"Lunch!" the girl exclaimed, still holding hands with both of them. "Magrobad!"

"Hmm? Ooh, I dunno, I think you'll need to be a bigger girl before we go to MgRonald..."

"No! Magrobad!"

Maou didn't know why she called it "bad," but either way, her obsession with MgRonald today was almost disturbing. "You ever take her there?" he asked Emi.

"No, but it's like she immediately picks up on the scent of fast food whenever we run into it. Not just MgRonald, either."

"The scent...?"

This rang a bell with Maou. When she'd first met Kisaki, the first words out of Alas Ramus's mouth were "You smell like Daddy!"

"Hey, Alas Ramus?"

"Yehh?"

"Why do you wanna eat at MgRonald so bad, anyway?" he asked, out of curiosity.

The answer from Alas Ramus's lips couldn't have been clearer.

"It smells like Daddy!"

"..."

Maou and Emi looked at each other in silence.

"Hey, Mommy? Can we all sleep in Daddy's house?" their child innocently asked.

"...Uh, let's eat first, okay?" Emi listlessly countered.

"Hey, Emi?"

"What?"

"Did that answer disappoint you?"

"...Huh?"

Maou's completely absurd question made Emi turn her head back in disbelief. Maou, for his part, looked just as flustered, as if not expecting that reaction.

"Oh, no, I just... Alas Ramus has been pretty much all about me today, so I thought you might be getting jealous, or..."

"...Look, I'm not *that* self-centered, all right? Oh, hey, there's a map here. Let's go look for someplace to eat, okay?"

"Uh, sure."

The shopping center directory was surrounded by several other families happily discussing the potential lunch suggestions among themselves.

"...I mean, of course she'd like you a lot. You gave her the first home she ever knew in this world."

"Y-yeah..."

"I'm just freaking out right now," came the matter-of-fact reply, "because I'm not sure whether being the Hero should come first, or being her 'mommy' should. That's all... Which of these do you think Alas Ramus could eat at?"

Each of the restaurant listings had a few sample photos and dish descriptions. Emi stared at them like nothing was amiss.

"Hmm. Well, sorry. Guess it doesn't really matter which one *I* put first, compared to you... How 'bout some soba noodles?"

"I don't need you feeling sorry for me, thanks. Besides, we've already been over this ...Ooh, that soba joint's pretty expensive. All the meals come with tempura, too."

"Already been over what? ...Tempura, huh? Hmm..."

"What do you think I mean? ...Can you even afford to eat out anyway? What's your budget?"

"Yeah, I got some money to work with. I get kind of a spending allowance every month outta my salary, and Ashiya gives me three hundred yen to buy something with whenever I go to work. Usually I save that up if I don't use it, so I got enough to feed me and Alas Ramus some tempura, anyway... Wait, was *that* what you meant?"

"What, about lunch?"

"No, I mean, I think we were talking about something more serious just now."

"Oh, that. I just figured it was better left unsaid. No point reminding you about it anyway... Yeah, I'm kinda sick of pasta for lunch anyway, so..."

"What? Just say it, man."

"Magrobad!" Alas Ramus erupted in joy, her eagle eyes spotting the MgRonald logo among the restaurant listings. The gesture made Emi smile a little as she glanced at Maou to her side.

"Like, if you're going to put being Daddy over being Devil King... If you're willing to give up on world conquest and live here in Japan for the rest of your life, then I wouldn't have any reason to be as stubborn as I am right now."

That was enough to sufficiently jog Maou's memory. The evening encounter at that one Sasazuka intersection after work. How did Emi see that incident? Why did she doggedly pursue the Devil King all the way to another world to take his life, only to say "If you're *willing* to live out life as a bright, happy young man in this world, I'm perfectly willing to not kill you"?

And that was even before Alas Ramus. It was just the Devil King and the Hero. Two sworn enemies. What did Emi *really* think about this new thing connecting them together? Clearly, the idea of them being seen as husband and wife physically sickened her. But what about the idea of her being the mother of a young girl?

"...Hey."

"What?"

"Y'know, if you ask the cashier at MgRonald, they'll cook up a batch of fries with no salt for you. How 'bout we give Alas Ramus some of those?"

"Huh? Where'd *that* come from?"

"It's probably gonna be packed in there, so how 'bout we get something to go and head over here?"

Ignoring Emi's question entirely, Maou placed his finger on a point in the Seiseki-Sakuragaoka area map next to the restaurant list.

"Hey, Alas Ramus?"

"Yehh?" came the reply. Maou gradually picked up the child until she was at eye level with him.

"Wanna go on a picnic?"

✳

"Geez, this is strong!"

Emi put a hand to her head to keep her hair from being blown around in the wind.

"Riverrrr!"

"Whoa, pretty big, huh?"

The three of them were at the banks of the Tama River, about a ten minute walk from Seiseki station. It was framed by a bridge to the right for the Keio rail line and featured a park, soccer field, tennis courts, and other equipment. From this vantage point, it was a sight to see.

"Why don't you think any of the trees here are being taken care of?" Emi idly asked.

"Maybe to keep a natural balance or something? I see a bunch of guys barbecuing on the other side, but I guess that's not allowed over here."

There was a large footbridge to the left, a large number of people cooking up a storm near the edge of the river.

"Daddy! Playground!"

Alas Ramus's eyes immediately turned to the playground equipment spread out down by the riverside.

"Sure," Maou replied to the girl on his back, "but let's get lunch taken care of first. I think there's a free bench over there."

He ran down from the path to the bank, straight for an old wooden bench just big enough for three people. It was strategically located under a bushy shade tree.

"...You know what a playground is, Alas Ramus?" asked an astonished Emi. "I don't think I've ever taken you to one before."

"Yeah, I think Ashiya and Suzuno took her to one near my apartment a few times when she was there."

"Mommy! Swings! I wanna go on the swings!"

Alas Ramus was about ready to leap right over Maou's shoulders for a chance at the swings.

"Huh," Emi observed as Alas Ramus swiveled around, squealing at everything around her. "I like to think I take her out a lot, but I'm at work all the time, so she's usually inside my body. Maybe I'm getting too stressed out. I should probably take a few shifts off..."

"Ah, don't bother. If things are going good now, then it's fine."

Maou sat Alas Ramus down on the bench and handed her the bag containing their MgRonald lunch. She grasped it eagerly, clutching it to her body.

"Magrobad!"

"I mean," he continued, "it'd be great if we could be with her twenty-four hours a day. But we both gotta work to make money, so that's not gonna happen. Hell, I had hardly any time to play with her even when she was staying in Devil's Castle. She was pretty much in Ashiya's and Suzuno's hands the whole time... Hold your hands out, okay, Alas Ramus? We need to wipe them down before you can eat."

He crouched down and wiped the child's pudgy hands with a towel he bought at the convenience store before looking up at Emi.

"Siddown," he said. "You're eating, right?"

"...Yeah."

Emi placed herself down next to Alas Ramus, an astonished look on her face.

"Oof," Maou grunted as he sat on the other side and looked down at the girl. "Okay, Alas Ramus, what do we say before we eat?"

"Okeh! Tink youuuuuu!"

Before anyone else could respond, her hands were into the small MgRonald bag handed to her. One of them extracted a handful of fries from the container within.

"Magrobad!"

There was nothing but an order of small fries inside. Beyond that, they chose a few tempting-looking to-go *onigiri* rice balls from an adjacent restaurant. It was Emi's suggestion.

"Here, Emi. Some tea."

Maou thrust a hundred-yen bottle of tea at her. Emi took it after a moment of hesitation, opened it up, and brought it to her lips.

"...Oh, this is good."

She checked the bottle. It was an unfamiliar brand from an even less familiar bottler.

"Yeah?" Maou laughed to himself as he opened up a bottle of his own. "I really liked that stuff. They sold it in convenience stores starting in the early spring, but I guess it didn't sell at all 'cause it disappeared pretty quick. Lately I've been seeing two-fer sales at the hundred-yen shop for fifty yen each. Better enjoy it before it disappears in the fall, huh? ...Hey, you drink some tea, too, Alas Ramus. All those fries are gonna make you thirsty."

"Mnngh...okehhh," Alas Ramus mumbled, mouth full of salt-free French fries. There was just enough space left inside for her to enjoy a swig or two from the bottle.

"...Man," Emi said. "You really *do* look like father and daughter." There was no other way for her to describe the scene before her—a summer day spent under the shade, a young father giving some tea to his daughter to help wash down their lazy lunch.

"It'd be nice if we could be, yeah."

"...What?"

Was that in response to Emi's observation? She couldn't tell for a moment.

"Besides, you're every part a mother to her, aren't you?"

"Uh... Well, I mean, I..."

And was *that* meant as a compliment?

"It's not like I'm avoiding thinking about all of this stuff, Emi. Like, how much longer can we be with Alas Ramus? Or is she gonna..."

The sounds of families playing in the playground below seemed tantalizingly far away.

"...is she gonna go away on her own volition sometime?"

"...Devil King..."

"Pfft!" Alas Ramus said, finally washing down the last of the fries. "Mommy! Oniiri!"

"Oh, sure," came the distracted reply as Emi took out a rice ball with pickled radish inside and presented the package to her.

"Wow, starting with radish, huh? Pretty hard-core choice."

"I like rar-ish!" she cried out as she started making the rice ball a thing of the past.

"...I guess she likes pretty much anything the color of Malchut," Emi explained.

"...Oh?" Maou laughed.

Alas Ramus had a preference—a yen, if you will—for anything bright yellow in color. It was the color controlled by Malchut, one of the other Yesod seeds from the tree of Sephirot and apparently a good friend of the Yesod seed she was a part of.

It made for a complex family tree—a half-angel Hero, a demonic overlord, and the personification of a potential planet. And it was clear as day to both of them that this family wasn't going to proceed along like any human-driven one.

"...Well, so what?"

For once in his life, Maou looked straight into Emi's eyes.

"It's not like stewing over it's gonna solve anything. There's no way we can just cast Alas Ramus away at this point, and...like, if you don't feel like using your holy sword to cut me in two or anything, there's no point thinking about what happens if she leaves us. It's just a waste of energy."

"...!"

Something about how clearly he laid out the situation for her robbed Emi of all speech. She had spent years polishing her sword skills in order to run one through the Devil King's heart someday. It was the whole reason she bore the holy sword in the first place. And now Alas Ramus called it home. Killing Maou with it would mean quite literally dousing Alas Ramus in the blood of her "daddy."

"I… Look, that doesn't mean I've given up on slaying you…!"

She hadn't given up. And she hadn't forgiven the Devil King for anything. Emi tried to summon her boldness, just so she could be sure that was understood by all parties involved. But the easygoing smile remained on Maou's face.

"You don't have to remind me, man. I'm not trying to take advantage of this whole deal to mess around with you or anything. Whoa, Alas Ramus, don't put a death grip on it or anything! Ahh, you're making it all fall apart!"

"Agh! You're getting bonito all over the place!"

This was what Maou got for trying to have a serious conversation for a change. Alas Ramus's love for all things topped with bonito flakes made her destroy the entire rice ball.

"Eesh," Maou lamented. "Here, lemme have that for a sec. Hey, Emi, you still got those chopsticks that came with it?"

"Yeah. Please don't squeeze those rice balls so hard again, okay, Alas Ramus? Here, say aah…"

"Aaaaaah!"

Emi gathered the rescued pieces of rice ball into the original container, plucked the tiny pieces up with the chopsticks, and brought them to Alas Ramus's mouth.

"Now it's both of us, huh?" Maou said. "It makes the whole Devil King and Hero thing seem moot by comparison."

"…"

Emi pretended to be too focused on feeding Alas Ramus to listen. Something about agreeing with that statement severely pained her. But Maou didn't seem to be seeking commentary on it. Instead, she picked off the rice grains sticking to Alas Ramus's clothes and shouted into the air:

"Man, this is nice weather, huh?"

✳

"Whew," Maou breathed as he stretched out atop the Sasazuka station platform. "What a marathon this wound up being!"

"…"

Even at six in the evening, the summer sun was bright as always. Yet Alas Ramus was fast asleep in Emi's arms. They had spent the rest of the afternoon watching the magical girl run herself ragged around the playground, completely forgetting about their original objective. She had fallen into a deep sleep on the train ride back.

A fairly constant breeze ran along the riverbanks, but the heat had still all but exhausted Maou and Emi. They were so spent, in fact, that they boarded the local train back to Sasazuka so they'd be guaranteed a seat.

"Well, Emi, you mind taking the pamphlets with you back home? I gotta explain everything to Ashiya, so…"

"…"

It would have been easier for Emi to leave the local train and switch out at Meidaimae station. She stayed on until Sasazuka entirely because Maou asked her to.

After a day spent fruitlessly casing the Seiseki shops, the two of them had begun talking about purchasing that first (quite expensive) set they looked at. But as long as they were both pitching in for this—as Maou put it—he had to run it by Ashiya first, or else there'd be hell to pay.

Emi was exasperated at the idea that the Devil King couldn't buy a single thing without his lackey's permission, but not even she was expecting an immediate purchase. They both needed some time to consider this.

What chagrined her about all this was the fact that, thoroughly exhausted, Maou fell asleep on the way home. And ever since he woke up at Sasazuka, Maou was concerned about how angry Emi seemed about something. She was offering no response to anything he said.

Then he noticed in the white evening sunlight that there was a sheen of light red over Emi's face. It was pretty sunny by the river, he supposed.

"Hey, did you forget to put some suntan lotion on? Your face is all red."

"...Look," she rumbled, her voice like an icicle chilled to absolute zero running through his heart. "I can't believe... I can't believe..."

"Um?"

And now she was shaking. Why? The anger much have been what made her eyes twinkle at that moment, as she brought her head close to his and opened her mouth, ready to spew fire with it.

"I can't believe you leaned on me that whole time!! You bastard!!"

"Huhh? Oh. Did I?"

This was news to Maou, having conked out almost immediately upon sitting down. But it must have been true. Emi wasn't one to lie without reason.

"Don't 'did I?' me! Can you believe how humiliating it was when this old lady got on the train at Sakurajosui station and started going on like 'Oh, what a fine couple you folks are!'?"

"Oh? Well...huh."

Now Emi's face was a brighter red. But she still had the discretion to keep her voice down, keeping Alas Ramus asleep and content. If her hands were free at all, she likely would've started choking Maou on the spot.

"I-I tried pushing you away with my shoulder, but every damn time the train stopped, you'd lean back on me again! I thought I was gonna die of embarrassment!"

"Um. Well. Sorry?"

"I was all set to abandon you at Meidaimae, too, you know! But you were asleep, and Alas Ramus was, too, and I didn't know what to... Aggggh! I hate you!"

"People're looking, people're looking," Maou hissed through his teeth, feeling the heat emanating from Emi's face during her ever-louder diatribe. "You're gonna wake up Alas Ramus, so...just calm down a sec, okay? Take a deep breath. I'll hold her for you."

"I...I *am* calm," Emi protested as she handed Alas Ramus to the man. She turned her back to him, stretching out to loosen up her body after her extended session on the train being a prop for him. As she did:

"Ah!"

"Ooh?"

"...Oh."

She made eye contact with someone. Both of them, along with Maou, froze.

"Wow, Maou, Yusa, and Alas Ramus?"

It was Chiho Sasaki, in her school uniform and giving the three of them a look that resembled a pigeon who had just been shot with a BB gun.

"Um, Chi?"

"H-hello there, Chiho..."

Neither of them ever imagined they would run into Chiho *now*, of all times.

"What are you guys doing here?" Chiho asked as calmly as possible.

"Oh, um, we were...just doing some shopping."

"Shopping?"

"Y-yeah," Emi stammered. "I needed to get something for Alas Ramus, but I...I couldn't decide by myself, so..."

"Oh? Yeah, I'll bet. It must be quite an adjustment to make, her moving to your place."

Chiho knew all about Alas Ramus, of course, so it wasn't exactly devastating news to see Maou and Emi in the same place together. But:

"...fffhhh...ngh."

Alas Ramus chose that moment to wake up in Maou's arms, her sleepy eyes taking in all of Chiho before her. Her parents, sensing her stirring a few moments before it actually happened, felt chills down their spines.

"Oh, hello there, Alas Ramus! Did you have a good time out today?"

"Yeah!" the girl cheerfully replied. "I went on a picnic with Mommy and Daddy!"

"Oh, a pic…nic…huh?" Chiho turned toward the couple.

"Yawwwn… I played a whole lot. And I'm gonna sleep with Mommy 'n' Daddy…tonight…mmm."

It was as if the still-not-quite-awake Alas Ramus was picking the exact words out of her quiver to make Chiho freeze in place.

"Wow, um…you, and Maou, and Yusa…?"

"Wait! No! It's not like that, Chiho!"

"Calm down, Chi! You know there's no way we could sleep together!"

But, judging by Chiho's complete lack of a reaction, their protests seemed to be falling on deaf ears.

"We…" Alas Ramus began. "We bought a futon…mmph…"

"A…futon…?"

"Chiho! Chiho, snap out of it!"

"Y-Yusa, are you and…and Maou making a real…a real fam—"

"Of course not, Chi! Why would I ever want a woman like *this* in my family?!"

"Yeah! The same goes for me, too!"

"Huhh? Mommy? Daddy?"

"A-Alas Ramus? No, um, Mommy and Daddy aren't arguing or anything, so…"

"So the three of you were out shopping for futons? Yusa, you aren't actually moving into his apartment, are you? You're gonna be a real family now?!"

"Chiho! Get ahold of yourself! We can explain everything!"

"Mommy, Daddy, stop fight…fight…*waaaaahhh!!*"

This exercise in torture for the Hero and Devil King continued for ten or so minutes afterward.

"Oh… So it's just a futon for Alas Ramus to sleep on during her stay?"

It ended only with the intervention of an exasperated Ashiya, who happened into the station just a moment too late to avoid the entire headache. His explanation of Maou's activities for the day as they walked to Devil's Castle was finally enough to put Chiho's mind at ease. Maou and Emi staggered along behind the two of them, still exhausted, with Alas Ramus taking up the child seat on Dullahan II as Ashiya wheeled it forward.

"Boy, that sure was a surprise, though," Chiho continued. "I mean, you guys really did look like a family back at the station…"

"Don't say it."

"Oh, don't say it…"

"…Wow, that was almost in stereo," Chiho chuckled as she heard the mutterings from behind her.

"Well, Your Demonic Highness? How did the shopping journey go?"

"Yeah, about that… I wanted to discuss things with you a little, so that's why I've got Emi along with me."

Ashiya's eyebrows shot downward. "…Cost-related things, I would imagine?"

"I think it'd be best to buy her something decent," interjected Chiho. "I heard that the way babies sleep can affect their bone structure and stuff."

"Yeah," Maou added, "so I figured we could talk about that and other things once we get home. By the way, Ashiya, who were you talking to just now?"

It was no mere coincidence that Ashiya had come across the group at the station. He was there because he was using one of the public phone booths out front.

"Oh, no one important. I merely needed to confirm an appointment with an acquaintance of mine." Ashiya turned the corner to Villa Rosa Sasazuka, one of its windows illuminated. "Bell was quite concerned over whether the two of them could manage a shopping trip without it devolving into an argument."

"No fighting, Mommy 'n' Daddy!" declared Alas Ramus from her bicycle throne, a stern look on her face as she turned around at her parents. Mommy and Daddy each let out defeated sighs in response.

"She has a point," Chiho commented. "It'd be best for everyone if we can keep on getting along for good, you know?"

"I am not sure I can entirely agree with that, Ms. Sasaki," the Great Demon General in attendance dutifully replied.

❅

"I *so* don't wanna go to work," Emi uncharacteristically grumbled as she battled the waves of morning commuters around Shinjuku station.

The entire group wound up having dinner at Suzuno's place the previous night, Emi staving off Alas Ramus's repeated demands to stay at Devil's Castle long enough to get her back to her apartment. Ashiya was more than a little disapproving of the futon's price, but—thanks in no small part to Chiho's convincing—it looked like the demons were ready to commit to a Torikawa purchase.

Emi figured she would have to report all this to Rika in order to avoid any more prying questions, even though she knew Rika would pepper her with them no matter what she tried. The thought didn't fill her with cheer.

She was still trying to figure out some way to dodge the topic by the time she reached her assigned office cube.

"…Rika?"

Rika was adjacent to her, staring into space. It was very unusual behavior for her, slack-jawed and unfocused, given how much of a morning person she usually was.

"Rika? You there?"

"………………………Oh! Hey, Emi."

Her reaction time was suffering.

What happened to her? She's a completely different person from yesterday.

"Hey, uh, remember the futon thing I told you about, Rika?"

"Futon……? What about it?"

It was a terminal case. She pounced upon the topic like a hyena yesterday, and now she couldn't be more disinterested. Emi began to feel concerned—this airheaded act was nothing like her usual ebullient personality.

"Hey, uh, are you feeling all right?"

"I…I don't think I, like, even know anymore."

"Huh?"

"Um, Emi?" Her whisper was almost lost in the morning bell.

"Wh-what?"

"Do you think it was always like this back before cell phones? Always so, like, frustrating?"

"I…I don't really know…"

"Ahh, I'm sorry. It's no big deal. Better get to work, huh?"

Rika slipped on her headphone mike, the listlessness still clear in her voice.

"I know things are pretty complicated for you, too, Emi…"

"Y-yeah?"

"But it's pretty important that you have someone to talk to, you know? Like, when you're trying to make up your mind about something."

There was no doubt in Emi's mind that whatever troubled Rika was intertwined in that remark. She didn't have time to inquire further. The first call of the day was already on her computer.

"…Thank you for calling the DokoDemo customer support center. This is Yusa speaking. How can I help you?"

The awkwardness that began the day was beaten down by both of their workaday responsibilities, and it quickly fell out of sight.

A FEW DAYS BEFORE: THE TEENAGER IS A PART-TIMER!

The cold wind, blowing through a window someone had left open, blew the small piece of paper out of her hand and onto the floor.

"Oop!"

The owner hurriedly stood to pick it up. There was nothing personally embarrassing written on it, but it was still nothing she wanted to show anyone. Her chair clattered against the wooden floor as she bent over.

"Ah!"

Then she looked up, following the other hand that grabbed it before her.

"Hmm…"

It belonged to her friend, eyebrows arched as she studied the note's content.

"Wh-whoa! Kao!" the owner said, calling her friend by her nickname as she tried to snatch it back. "Don't read it!"

"Uh-uh. I'm keeping it," came the childish reply.

"Kao!"

"Sasachi, what is going on here?"

"What?"

Sasahata North High School, classroom 2-A. Kaori Shoji, the owner's best friend both in class and in the after-school clubs she was part of, glumly thrust the paper back into the hands of "Sasachi."

"You got at least an eighty-five in everything!"

"Agh! Not so loud!"

"Oh, what's the big deal telling people about *that*?" Kaori said, slipping behind her friend and putting her in a playful headlock. "I averaged like sixty or below across the board! You just sit there like a good little girl all day, and you're, like, head of the class! Why can't you lend me some of those brains, huh?"

"Agh! I…ergh…hey! Kao, Kao?"

"Oh?"

"…I thought I kind of *did*, Kao."

"Oh… Oh?"

Kaori turned her head back. Her friend didn't let the opportunity go untaken. She snatched back the paper containing the results from the mock exam the teachers cruelly held right after spring break, placed it on her desk, and slipped out of Kaori's grasp. With a whirl, she grabbed Kaori's left arm from below, swung both it and herself behind her back, and squeezed a little.

"Ah-ha-ha! Agh, Sasachi! Not from the side! That's cheating!"

Restricting her friend's movements, Sasachi began tickling Kaori's side. "I told you everything that'd be on the test, didn't I?" she said. "I cut into my study time to help you out, didn't I? What were you doing after club all spring break?"

"Ah-ha-ha-ha-ha-ha, no, no, uncle, uncle, I can't take any more!"

Kaori's legs swung up and down as she attempted to withstand the attack. Her friend, not being that much of a sadist, let go.

"Phew… I-I was studying, all right?" Kaori said, twirling her hair as she caught her breath. "I mean, you're a really good tutor and everything, but I kinda had a time crunch going on."

Kaori was far from a bad student. But if that was how she fared, Sasachi feared for the worst when it came to her other friend. The one approaching them right now, in fact.

"Holy crap, Sasaki!" he exclaimed in surprise as he goggled at the test results on her desk. "You're, like, sixty points ahead of the curve!"

"Oh, Kohmura…"

Yoshiya Kohmura sat one desk ahead of her. He and Kaori had been Sasaki's classmates from their first year of high school, as well as her companions at the *kyudo* archery club. They were all next to each other in the Japanese-language alphabetical order, and for now—before seats would be reassigned for the new semester—they were all seated in the same column of desks.

"How'd *you* do, Yoshiya?" Kaori asked.

"Oh, me? I pretty much blew English and Japanese," he declared, "but I made it over fifty points in everything else, I think."

"Sweet! I beat Yoshiya!"

"Kohmura..." Sasaki's shoulders drooped as Yoshiya pumped his fist in the air.

Their classmates, all well familiar with the trio over the past year, showed zero restraint with their comments. "Ooh, man, Chi's freakin' out again." "Kohmura blew it? Man, that sucks. There's hardly anyone in the *kyudo* club, too..."

"Is Sasaki here? Chiho Sasaki?"

Chiho dejectedly raised her head at the sudden voice. At the door Mr. Ando, her homeroom and classical Chinese teacher, was beckoning to her.

"Here, could you pass these out for me?"

She was hardly class president, but for some reason, he handed over little jobs like these to Chiho pretty often. This time, it was a stack of stapled paper, three sheets per staple. The topmost one read "Year-Two Parent-Teacher Conferences." It was April, right at the beginning of Chiho's second high school year. There was still a chill to the wind, and while spring was in the air, nobody wanted to let go of their winter uniform sweaters yet.

For her, the year was starting just like they all had since middle school—without much in the way of new excitement.

✳

"Hey, why do you have to be all depressed about Yoshiya's crappy scores?" Kaori asked the down-in-the-dumps Chiho. "It's not like he actually tried to prep for it or anything... 'Course, I guess I *did* study and my scores still weren't great, so I don't have much room to judge."

There was something creepy to the sense of bragging pride Yoshiya approached his failure-level scores with. But Chiho was concerned about other matters. "I dunno," she said, "it just makes me worry about what happens when the tests actually count. Like with the next midterms. I'd like to think he'll be okay, but..."

"Yeah," Kaori replied, a bit of concern showing through for her as well. But then, she pointed at the edge of Chiho's lips. "Oh, hey, Sasachi, you got some ketchup right here."

Chiho used a paper napkin to wipe the stain away. It was from the burger she was having at the MgRonald by Hatagaya rail station, conveniently located on the way home from school. She and Kaori went there a lot after school or extracurricular activities. It wasn't like Chiho was some kind of fast-food gourmet, but it always seemed to her that what they cooked up at *this* particular MgRonald was a lot better than the other quick-service joints—even other MgRonalds.

"I mean," Chiho said after wiping up, "if that had been a real test, Kohmura would've been put on academic probation. He'd be banned from club activity, too, and that'd suck not just for him, but everyone else in *kyudo*."

"Yeah, that's a good point," Kaori commiserated as she nibbled on a French fry. "We're the only sophomore students in the club right now, and if we lost the only sophomore *guy* in the club, we're gonna have a lot of trouble fielding freshman members."

Among the city public schools in the area, Sasahata North High was on the more advanced side when it came to academics. It had even sent a student to the prestigious Tokyo University in the past. As a result, studying was the primary focus of a lot of the student body—and if you were scored in the bottom-fourth percentile in three of the regular examinations, you were temporarily banned from sports and extracurriculars, except in exceptional cases like national championships.

The *kyudo* club that Chiho, Kaori, and Yoshiya joined last year was rather sparsely populated. If it weren't for them, in fact, it would've been a serious candidate for disbanding. Considering that not too many high schools in Japan had dedicated archery facilities, the Sasahata North club got to enjoy some pretty nice perks—but not only was *kyudo* unpopular, but also the monetary requirements for getting into the sport put it at a disadvantage compared to others.

For the time being, the club consisted of the three of them, plus a single senior pair, a guy and girl. They had a teacher as an advisor, but that was pretty much on paper only—he had no *kyudo* experience. Instead, they were led by old alumni and rank-holding archers in the area who volunteered with them several times a month, but who could help them improve their skills only so much.

Thus, if they couldn't get at least three male first-year students to sign up this year, they wouldn't even be able to enter official boys' competitions any longer. As a direct result, the club wasn't exactly a contending force in the *kyudo* scene. Sasahata North had yet to so much as smell a national championship berth. Their historical best performance was a quarterfinal run at the Tokyo city tournament over a decade ago.

All this meant that if Yoshiya's scores were failure-level on three midterm subjects, he'd be out of the club in an instant. That'd affect the morale of whatever freshman students they attracted—to say nothing of Chiho and Kaori themselves. And with local tournaments coming up soon, he wouldn't be able to get in the practice he needed to have half a chance at going anywhere.

Chiho didn't feel any intense drive to devote every waking moment of her teenage years to archery, like the star of some guts-and-glory sports manga. But if she was devoting herself to this one sport, she felt a responsibility to show up at competitions fully prepared, at the very least. That was exactly why Kaori's middling performance in the mock exams came as such a shock to her. She had never been one to slack off like that, then blame it on some vague excuse like "I'm busy." At least, Chiho didn't think she was.

"I feel bad about that, you know?" Kaori said. "It's just…I don't wanna make excuses or anything, but I think the club's part of the reason I couldn't get everything I wanted out of your tutoring."

"Oh?"

Kaori placed her pouting face on the table. "I was actually working part-time during spring break."

"Oh, you were?"

This was news to Chiho. Sasahata North didn't have any rules against working, so she knew at least some of her classmates held after-school jobs. But hearing it from Kaori piqued her interest.

"What kind of job did you have?" Chiho leaned forward. "And what for, huh?"

"Well," Kaori replied, a little embarrassed, "I'm not really as good at archery as you are. I keep bending my arrows and stuff, and you know how spendy those bows can get."

"Oh, come on, I'm not *that* good, Kao…"

Chiho wasn't being modest for politeness' sake. She was just about at the point where she could hit a thirty-six-centimeter target at *kinteki* range, close range and about ninety feet away, but getting it straight on the bull's-eye still wasn't something she could deliberately try for. She and her two fellow club members were still beginners, only taking up the sport last year, so there wasn't any great difference in their respective performance levels.

"No," Kaori said, "but you don't mess up your arrows much at all anymore with *makiwara* training, you know?"

The *makiwara* practice targets made out of straw looked like they'd be kind to arrows at first glance, but unless you made a pretty clean strike on them, they could be murder on the cheaper arrows the club members used.

"Plus," she continued, "the practice arrows we've got at the club are just a little too big for my equipment. That's why I took a job: because I wanted some new stuff…and that's why I didn't really study too much of what you taught me. Sorry."

"Oh… I'm sorry. I guess I didn't know."

Once the initial surprise was gone, Chiho found herself viewing Kaori with a certain level of respect. She had never taken a job before, and that in itself made her a little more grown-up in her eyes.

"It's fine, it's fine! It was my choice anyway, Sasachi. Besides, you're getting better with those same practice arrows, so I'm telling you, you've got a lot more talent than me."

"Oh, I do not…"

Kyudo, like ice hockey, took some serious cash to participate in. Even at the student level, fifty thousand yen was the ballpark figure for assembling the equipment you needed, more than enough to give even Chiho pause. In her life, that kind of money just wasn't possible unless her parents were willing to help her out. It was a lucky thing that Sen'ichi, Chiho's father and a lifelong police officer, was proud of his girl for choosing a martial art as an extracurricular.

She was perfectly willing to work with whatever was cheapest, but her dad—a ranked kendo practitioner—would have none of it. "If you start cheap," he reasoned, "that'll stunt your improvement level later on." So he bought her the best equipment possible within the standard price range.

Chiho appreciated that, and she made sure all of her stuff was fully maintained. But like Kaori said, things like arrows and bowstrings were generally consumable goods, so the running costs for maintenance were nothing to sniff at. One could always purchase sturdier duralumin arrows, but since every archer's sense of balance in terms of string tension, standing position, and arrow weight was different, it was tough to assemble a full set of *kyudo* equipment on the cheap.

"…I'm pretty impressed, though, Kao."

"With what?"

"Like, I never even thought about working to earn the money for the right *kyudo* stuff."

Chiho chose the *kyudo* club mainly because she thought it looked pretty cool. She was in the choir in middle school, something Sasa-hata North didn't have. That meant she wanted to pick something else, and when she saw one of the senior members striking the styl-ized full-draw *kai* pose as he readied himself to shoot at the extra-curricular fair last year, something clicked with her. The bow he used in the demonstration wasn't the carbon-fiber type Chiho and her friends used—it was a beautiful bamboo bow, its clear whiteness penetrating into its very core.

"Ahh, it's nothing *that* impressive," Kaori groaned, interrupting Chiho's trip down memory lane. "I quit, anyway."

"Oh? Was it just a temp thing?" Chiho asked, still a little fuzzy on how part-time work *worked*.

"Nah," Kaori replied as she took a sip of orange juice. "I just quit 'cause the job sucked. It was at a diner."

"A diner?"

There were a ton of them around Hatagaya and Sasazuka, both chains and family-run places.

"Like, I don't want people calling me a quitter or anything, but I just could *not* do that any longer. The customers were *scary*, too."

"Really?"

"Yeah. My supervisor basically threw me in the deep end my third time in, even though I still didn't know all the stuff I needed to. You know the little computer pads they use to take down orders? There's, like, a ton of keys on that thing, and each of the buttons had, like, four different menu items associated with them. And then everything got switched out for some new spring ad campaign, so it took me forever to take orders."

"Huh," Chiho said, recalling the last time she was at a franchise diner. "But didn't you have one of those little In Training things on your name tag?"

Kaori rolled her eyes and shook her head. "Yeah, like customers give a crap about that. Did you look at the cashier's name tag when you ordered that just now?"

"Oh, I did actually. That guy with the black hair. You see him?

I remember it because it said MAOU on it. That's a pretty unusual name, you know? Plus it had B CREW on it, too."

Chiho took a look back at the counter. It was occupied by a man with black hair who looked like he had just stepped out of a MgRonald TV commercial.

"…Well, that's because you're special, Sasachi." Kaori turned her jaded eyes back to Chiho. "But it's like, if I'm still in training, why do people think I'd know what's in this or that kind of pasta, or how many calories are in a hot-fudge sundae or whatever? I've never even *seen* that stuff."

"Isn't that usually written in the menus?"

Without warning, Kaori stood up and pointed a defiant finger at Chiho.

"Yeah! Yeah, you'd think that, wouldn't you? But they never look! They *never* look. Like, they just toss the menu away and say, like, 'What do you think I should get?' As if I have any idea!"

"Wow… That bad, huh? 'Cause I don't think I've really seen that before when I'm shopping or going out or—"

Before Chiho could finish, Kaori leaned even further over the table. "Oh, you will if you stand there for six hours straight. Like, every single day! And that's just the easy stuff. Sometimes people helped themselves to the drink machine because they assume it's free. Then they got all pissy at me once I said it wasn't. Or they bitch about how the plates are all different from the last time they ate there. Like, what does telling *me* that accomplish?"

"Oh… Wow."

"But the worst was when the lunch rush came, and we were completely full with customers waiting for a seat. These business guys came in, and I told them to take a number and wait, and they were like 'We gotta wait? Why do we gotta wait?' Like, do they even know how a restaurant works?"

"…That's pretty rude, yeah."

It was hard for Chiho to believe, but Kaori wasn't the type to exaggerate for effect. That group must have actually existed.

"Yeah, isn't it? So I didn't know how to answer that, and then they got really riled up and were all like 'Let me speak to your manager.' So I did that, and then the manager got all pissed at me for interrupting her while she was busy!"

"Oh, no way."

"So then she disappeared, so it was just me and this other girl covering the entire dining area. Where I was at, the waitstaff had to make some of the dessert items on the menu instead of the cooks. I had, like, no training on any of that, but this guy just handed me a manual and ordered me to make a parfait for him. How was I gonna do *that*, huh? I didn't even know where anything was."

The rant continued on. She was forced to do things she had no experience with, then was yelled at when she inevitably messed them up. Her conniving coworkers gave her no support, even though they had all the time in the world. To her, at least, part-time work held no attractions at all.

Then a thought occurred to Chiho. "But they're gonna pay you, right? You quit before you were there a full month?"

"I think they will, yeah. I was still in my training period, and I only worked for, like, half a month, so it ain't gonna be that much. Ugh, it was just awful!"

Kaori pushed her now-empty MgRonald tray away from her and sunk into her seat. Just as she did, a voice rang out.

"Ma'am, I can take that tray for you if you like."

The two of them looked up. Each of them let out a tiny gasp. There was a woman there, dressed in a different uniform from the rest of the crew. "Beautiful" was the only to describe her. She was tall, her skin shiny and as flawless as a ceramic vase, with a voice low and inviting like a fashion model's. Given their conversation just now, Chiho couldn't help but look at her name tag. KISAKI: MANAGER, it read.

Kaori nodded silently in awe as Kisaki took the tray away and gave a light, polite bow as she went on her way. Chiho still had some fries and her drink on her tray, so the manager had given her a bit more time.

"Pretty lady, huh?" Kaori was still staring at her. "Maybe I would've lasted longer with her managing me. My boss at that diner practically did nothing unless there were customers to wait on, and then she yelled at me to find something to do when I wasn't busy. Like, why don't you try working a little, huh?"

She kept looking at the MgRonald manager until she disappeared behind the counter. Chiho chuckled at the display.

"Yeah, I keep hearing that working at a restaurant or a convenience store is hard enough as it is. They really shouldn't be making part-timers do work they don't know how to do. I mean, like I should talk, never having had a job before, but—"

"Oh, no, totally. Plus she kept yelling at me all the time, which didn't help my motivation any, but… Ah, screw it! It's all in the past now. I hope I never wait tables again for the rest of my life!"

After making the bold declaration, Kaori took some paper out of her school tote bag. It was the stapled set Mr. Ando made Chiho hand out earlier—a notice about the upcoming parent/teacher/student conferences, along with a survey.

"And really," she said, "how am I supposed to know what I wanna do with my life right now?"

The career guidance survey asked students to specify whether they intended to go to a university, a technical school, or right into the workforce after graduating high school, and why. Student responses would apparently be used to help guide the upcoming three-party conferences.

"You're totally going to college, aren't you, Sasachi?"

Chiho vaguely nodded. "Um…probably." The survey made her feel a little down as well. Two whole years of high school to go, and she was already being asked to consider the entire rest of her life.

"No way Yoshiya's gonna make it into any other school after this," Kaori flatly stated. "Me, though…I dunno. The one thing I do know is absolutely no food-service work. But what kinda reason should I even write down? I mean, I don't even know what I would major in if I went to college."

Chiho felt exactly the same way. Apart from the big names like Tokyo and Kyoto University, the only universities she was familiar with were the ones that placed high in the Ekiden relay races her father watched on TV every New Year's Day. But going to work right after high school? To someone like Chiho with zero work experience, that seemed even more alien and unfamiliar than college.

"Ooh, but maybe some talent scout would pick you up, huh, Sasachi? You're cute and your tits're huge, so I bet they'd snap you up if you walked around the Harajuku fashion district. Why don't you put down 'entertainment industry' in the survey?"

"Umm…"

Kaori was bound and determined to mention Chiho's chest to her at least once a day. They were a source of jealousy for many of her peers, even if Chiho herself saw absolutely no benefit to them. The bowstring would snap against them if she wasn't paying attention to her archery stance. She felt bad for how much the bras she had her mom buy her cost, and there was nothing very attractive about her size anyway. They hadn't caused her any shoulder pain yet, but she'd often find a blouse she liked that was sized perfectly for her arms and shoulders, but she still couldn't wear because the buttons wouldn't go over her bust or she would bulge out in odd and revealing ways.

"Oh, that's just silly," she protested as she took her own copy of the handout from her bag and stared at it. "We gotta be serious about this. Our parents are gonna look at it, too." .

Kaori brought a hand against her forehead. "Oh, geez, I forgot about that! Now I really don't know what to write…"

The sheet had a pretty large fill-in box meant for providing your reasons and motivations for your postgraduate choices. It made Chiho want to rub her forehead in frustration. She always struggled to reach so much as 80 percent of the required word count in composition class. The term itself—*career guidance*—had struck her with a sense of nameless dread ever since it first started popping up in middle school.

Chiho had taken and passed the exam to get into Sasahata North simply because it was close to her house and a good match for her academic skills. It wasn't because of some particular specialty subject she wanted to study there. That was exactly what she'd written in her postgrad survey back in middle school. It was a little too honest for her teacher at the time, who advised her to give a bit more suitable of a reason.

Kaori hadn't mentioned it, but she remembered some of her classmates writing about their desires to become film stars or professional athletes, only to be told by their parents and teachers not to write stupid things like that. And yet grown-ups would constantly gripe about "Oh, kids these days, they all want jobs in the government! Don't any of them have dreams any longer?" It sounded terribly hypocritical to her, encouraging children to dream big and shooting them down when they obliged. Plus, Chiho's policeman father was a government worker. Bluntly stating that his job was unimaginative, not worthy as a dream, made it sound like all would-be police officers were idiots in her mind. The whole career-guidance thing just seemed like a charade.

"It's not like I know what I wanna do, either…"

"Mm? How so, Sasachi?"

"Oh, I dunno…"

Chiho sometimes felt like the whole adult world was stacked against people like her. But it wasn't like she had some grand plan for her life she could reveal to people. It just wasn't there in her mind. It was easy to imagine graduating from college and finding a job at a good company somewhere, but given how the news kept going on about slowing growth and how hard it was to start a career in "*this* economy," she knew that scoring a decent job was about a lot more than high school test scores.

Some would-be know-it-alls on the Net even declared that a college degree didn't actually help you at all in the job market. So why did the big companies always prefer new hires from prestigious universities? It started to make less and less sense to her.

Chiho set the handout to the side of the table, picked up her drink, and glared at it distractedly as she brought the straw to her mouth. Then she noticed the paper place mat on her tray.

"...Huh. They're hiring part-time crewmembers."

They pretty much always were, it seemed like, judging by how often she had seen this place mat in the past.

"Sasachi?"

"Listen, Kao—you having that job; do you think that taught you stuff about life as a grown-up that you didn't get in school?"

"Oh, no way. I mean, pretty much all I learned was that work is a pain in the ass I can't wait to get out of."

She was right, no doubt, but to someone like Chiho who grew up wanting for nothing under a loving mother and father, it felt like Kaori, and her experience in a world Chiho knew nothing about, made her seem closer to adulthood than Chiho was.

"I was just thinking," Chiho began, "maybe if I found a job, too, that'd help me figure out what I wanna do with my life. Like, with work and all."

"Huhh?!" Kaori's eyes burst open. "No. No way, man. Don't do it! Didn't you listen to anything I just said?!"

"Yeah, but...I dunno, like, at least to get some better equipment like you were talking about..."

"Well, sure, I hate bugging my parents for money for arrows all the time, but what am I gonna do? Besides, with your grades, you could easily wait 'til college to get a job."

"Hmm... Maybe, but..."

She pictured that recent grad with the bamboo bow and arrow, the one who inspired her to take up *kyudo*. He probably didn't use that *all* the time, but with the right job and the right salary, a work of art like that could be hers, even. And if she learned more about working along the way, that was two birds with one stone.

"Hey, Sasachi, you're a smart girl, okay? And it's not like you're getting a crappy allowance or anything. You never really throw around your money anyway."

Kaori was clearly dead set against the idea.

"Well…I mean, I'm not trying to dive right into something, but…"

Kaori and Yoshiya kept going on about how smart Chiho was, but it wasn't like she was the top in her school or getting full-ride scholarship offers. Something in her wanted to try something new before it was *too late*, and she couldn't deny that the urge was growing.

Then—

"Ah!"

Chiho shouted out loud, too lost in thought to think about her surroundings. A bag carried by a passing businessman swung close by the table, the shoulder strap all twisted up against itself, and it knocked against the drink cup she had in her hand. It didn't hurt, but the impact caused her to let go. The paper had softened a little—she and Kaori had been sitting and chatting for a while by this point—and the fall caused the lid to pop right off upon hitting the table, immediately soaking her copy of the survey in lukewarm soda.

"Oooh…"

The businessman must have noticed the mistake he had made. But the shock didn't end there. When the two girls looked up, they were face-to-face with someone who clearly wasn't Japanese. He was a Western man, well built and with a bushy beard, and although he was saying something or other in rapid succession to the two of them, Chiho was too broken up over the handout to decipher any of it.

"Ooh, what should I do?"

"You all right, Sasachi?" a worried Kaori asked, just as unable to understand the foreigner as Chiho. "Oh, geez, your handout… That's, uh, that isn't bad, is it?"

"_____!"

All three parties involved knew something bad had just taken place, but nobody could get their ideas across to each other. The man, looking deeply troubled, offered a handkerchief to Chiho, even though her clothes were dry and the paper was already ruined. The two girls were lost—unsure what to do, what they should do, or even how to begin processing these events.

"Did you need some help, ma'am?" a young man intervened.

Chiho looked up at the familiar voice. It was the man with the black hair who took her order earlier, running up to their table between Kaori and the businessman. His attention was focused on the lake of warm soda on the table.

"Oh, are you all right? Are your clothes wet, or…?"

"Um, I'm fine…"

"No you aren't, Sasachi!" Kaori finally took a moment to lift the sopping paper from the puddle. "What're we gonna do with this handout?"

"Well, what *can* we do?" The paper was dripping in the air. "We can't towel it off or anything."

"_____!"

The man said something again. Chiho could tell it was English, but she was in no shape to conduct a conversation. She tried to formulate a "that's all right"–style response, based on the assumption that he was apologizing.

Then the employee with Maou on his name tag spoke up.

"Um, this man said he wanted to make this up to you somehow…"

"Oh…?"

"_____!"

"Like, 'I'm sorry I wasn't paying attention, so I want to make it up to you if I can.' Is that some kind of school thing you have there?"

"Y-yes, it's a career guidance handout," Kaori said in place of Chiho, who was too surprised to talk. The employee gave both of them a look, then started talking to the businessman in fluent English.

<"Okay, so those documents were for career guidance purposes at her school…">

<"Oh, really?"> The man scratched at his beard, clearly embarrassed.

"So, um, I apologize, but does your friend here have a copy of that same document?"

"Huh? Uhm, yeah, but why?"

"I'm sorry," the employee said apologetically, "but I couldn't help but hear you from over by the counter."

"Oh, uh, sorry we were so loud," Chiho replied, feeling almost as embarrassed as the businessman.

The employee meekly smiled at her. "How about we do this?" he said. "That document's just a regular old printout, right? If your friend hasn't filled in hers yet, I'd be happy to borrow it and have him make another copy at the convenience store nearby..."

"Ah...?"

"Uh...sure...?"

Both of them nodded, mouths agape. It was such an obvious solution, but they were in such a panic that it occurred to neither of them.

<"Actually, sir, they have another blank copy of it here. Would you mind maybe making another copy for them? There's a pay copier at the convenience store a few doors over.">

The businessman raised his hands, nodded, and said something.

"He asked if one of you could bring it over to the convenience store with him, since he didn't want to risk messing up the last good copy. I can come along with you, so if you don't mind making a little trip..."

"Oh, sure, absolutely." Kaori, now much calmer, nodded at the employee and stood up. "That guy'll pay for it?"

"He said he'd be willing to make a hundred copies if you wanted."

It was the kind of Hollywood-style good humor Chiho all but expected from the foreigner.

"Wait here, okay?" Kaori said. "I'll be right back."

"I'm going out on a customer errand!" the employee shouted to the female manager behind the counter as the three of them left.

Thanks to that Maou guy's quick thinking, things went astonishingly smoothly from the initial frenzy. She was getting her handout back after all, something that made her feel tremendously relieved. But that wasn't the end of it.

"Pardon me, miss…"

The beautiful manager went up to Chiho's table and gave her a refined bow.

"Did any of your clothing get wet, perhaps?"

"Oh, uh, no, it's all fine, ma'am."

"Ah, great. My apologies for all the trouble, though. Would you like me to bring you a new drink and fries?"

"Huh? Oh, you don't…"

Now Chiho was even more surprised. This manager had absolutely nothing to apologize for. Thanks to that Maou person, not only did she know the businessman apologized to her already, but she was also getting another handout, to boot. If anything, Chiho had to apologize for things erupting as they did. Getting another complete snack out of it just felt manipulative to her.

She tried to say as much to the manager, but was provided with a smile and a shake of the head instead.

"Our job here is to create the best environment we can for our customers to enjoy their meals. That's why it's our responsibility to make sure that any conflicts between customers can be solved as smoothly as we possibly can. It's only natural for Maou…for that crewmember, I mean, to step in and lend a hand."

Chiho turned back toward the door they all exited through.

"I do feel bad for getting your friend involved in all this, though. If you're going to be leaving soon, I'd be happy to provide your replacements at a later date, as long as you bring today's receipt with you. Would that work better for you today, miss?"

The manager's words were pure, unadorned, and completely sincere. Chiho had all but forgotten about the incident by now. Instead, she found herself moved by the employees working so selflessly for them—the man who used his fluent English to defuse the situation, and the woman whose apology was clearly something that came from the heart.

She didn't want to badmouth Kaori's old boss when she wasn't here to defend herself, but something about a workplace with these people around indicated to Chiho that she wouldn't have to worry about employees stabbing her in the back. Something about the way she put it—"creating an environment." Chiho thought working at MgRonald was just about making burgers and slinging them at customers. The concept suddenly seemed a lot fresher to her.

"My receipt…?" Chiho took out the receipt she had folded up and stuck in her wallet. Something on it caught her eye.

"Right," the manager said, pointing at it. "You can bring that back in anytime you like…" But Chiho's eyes were elsewhere—on the text at the far bottom: "HELP WANTED," followed by a phone number.

"Umm…"

"Yes?"

What Chiho had to say next, not to put too a fine a point on it, changed the trajectory of her life forever.

"Uh, this number here is just for this location, right?"

✳

"What? Working at the Mag?!"

"Kao, I told you, you're being too loud!"

"Whoa, you're gettin' a job, Sasaki?!"

The following day at school, Chiho told her friends Kaori and Yoshiya that she had applied for a position at the MgRonald in Hatagaya. Both of them immediately shot to their feet at the news.

"After that thing that happened yesterday and all?"

"That wasn't MgRonald's fault," Chiho said. "That guy apologized to us, like, a million times, too."

"Well, don't say I didn't warn you, all right? 'Cause when it gets bad, it gets real bad out there."

"Hey, Sasaki's made of a lot different stuff from you, Shoji, y'know? How 'bout we all go there to eat once they hire her?"

"Oh, come on, Yoshiya, quit talkin' out your ass."

Chiho stepped in to stop the two of them from staring each other down any further.

"But, hey, why d'you want a job all of a sudden anyway?" Yoshiya asked.

"Well," Chiho began as she fought off the marauding Kaori, "you know that handout yesterday, right? I just figured, right now, I can't really say anything about what I want to do and be sure I'm telling the truth at all. I just figured working a little and earning some money could help me learn more about work, and life, and stuff."

"Doubt it."

Kaori scrunched up her face. Chiho deflected it with a chuckle: "Plus, it's the same motive you had, Kao. I wanna get some money for archery equipment…and some other stuff."

"Oh, totally. Wish I had some."

"Yoshiya, if you started working, you'd be failing a lot more than just two subjects."

"…Yeaaaaaah. Maybe."

Yoshiya usually let it slide whenever Kaori berated his study skills. This time, though, it seemed to Chiho that he took it personally a bit.

"I mean," he continued, "whether I'm failing two classes or twenty of 'em, you're about the only two people who get angry at me about it. Actually, I'm kinda jealous of you, Sasaki…gettin' all serious about this career guidance stuff and everything."

"…Kohmura?"

Chiho could sense the loneliness behind the words.

"If you realize that, you could actually try studying for a change…"

Kaori didn't care.

"Ah, it's not like they'll be at conferences anyway. Like, I don't even know if Mom 'n' Dad are gonna bother showing up or not."

"Huh? Really?"

For a school like Sasahata North that treated college prep seriously, these conferences—although they could be scheduled with a lot of leeway—were de facto mandatory for parents.

"Yeah, they don't really give a shit about me either way."

"Oh?"

"Huh?"

Yoshiya uttered the statement so quickly, it took a few moments for it to register with the girls.

"Oh, but hey, Sasaki," he continued, "if they hire you, I'm gonna get Shoji and the rest of the class and we're gonna bum-rush you during lunch, so watch out for us, okay?"

"Kohmura! Stop being stupid!" Kaori shouted.

"Aw, c'mon, Shoji! It's fun bothering your friends at work! You never even told me where you were working, either. You're such a party pooper!"

"Yeah, because I knew you were gonna do *that* to me! That job was stressful enough without getting your dumb ass involved in it!"

"Uh, h-hang on, guys," Chiho timidly said. "I haven't been hired yet, so..."

Reflecting for a moment, Chiho remembered that she was far from the only Sasahata North student who hung out at that MgRonald. The idea of her classmates seeing her in a different context from the classroom struck her as a tad embarrassing for reasons she couldn't quite express.

"Man, you're gonna totally regret telling Yoshiya in a few days, Sasachi."

"It's fine! I don't care if people look at me! If they hire me, I'm gonna be there to work anyway!"

"Sweet! Lemme know once they do, okay?"

This was starting to get weird. Chiho started to regret bringing up the topic at all, even though her resolve to work remained strong as ever. She had called the number immediately upon arriving home the previous night, surprising Kisaki the manager more than a little when she came on the phone. They agreed to an interview the very next day.

She already had her parents' permission—"as long as you keep your grades up," they had said. And now, in class, her hands were fidgeting with the résumé in her bag, one she had created the previous evening after reading through some sample guides.

✳

Maybe it was because they had already met, but being greeted by the manager that evening made Chiho far less nervous than she expected. Here they were now, one-on-one in the staff room, a place that had been off-limits to her just a day ago.

Mayumi Kisaki, manager of this MgRonald location, introduced herself to Chiho once again, using the same polite speech she applied to her customers.

"Let me take a few moments to look over your résumé," she said as she took it from her hands. That was the trigger that finally made Chiho start to sweat. Were there any spelling errors? Anything weird that stood out too much?

"...All right," the manager nodded after a few moments as she placed the paper on the desk. "Ms. Sasaki?"

"Y-yes?"

"You wrote in there that you wanted to build 'experience in society' through part-time work."

"Uh, yeah... Is that a problem?"

"Oh, no. Not a *problem*, no." Kisaki looked Chiho square in the eyes. "Is there some pressing need, perhaps, driving you to get this experience?"

"Um...a need?"

The unexpected question threw Chiho for a loop. She had written that, all right, and she'd even meant it. Kisaki, perhaps sensing her confusion, smiled a little.

"Oh, I was just wondering. I know Sasahata North is one of the better public schools in this neighborhood, and you're in one of the sports clubs, too. I was just wondering why you want to build this kind of experience so badly that you're willing to sacrifice your free time away from school to take a demanding part-time job."

"Well...um..."

"Don't worry. It's just you and me in here, Ms. Sasaki. If you're willing to tell me, I'd love to hear why."

"..."

Kisaki turned toward Chiho, her office chair creaking under her weight as she brought her face a bit closer. Her eyes gave Chiho an inkling of what her question really meant.

"It's, like, my future career..."

"Mmm?"

"I don't really know what I want to do with myself."

"Ah, your future? Whether you want to go to college or find a job out of high school?"

"Right. My friend was telling me about her job, and she told me about a lot of stuff that I never would've been able to learn about in school. I've been studying really hard since middle school, but it's, like, the more I think about my future career path, the more it just totally confuses me. So then yesterday, when you came up to me..."

"When I did?"

"You talked about 'creating an environment' for people and it was like... I dunno, I used to just think of MgRonald as a place that sold burgers and fries to people, but the way you put it made it seem like work's about a lot more than what you'd really see from the outside... It's kind of hard to explain."

Chiho knew that her words were just as jumbled up and inscrutable as her feelings on the subject. But Kisaki stood still and nodded, never trying to hurry her along.

"But anyway, I started thinking about what working was really like, and when you said I could get the same stuff again if I brought in my receipt, it was, like, *wow*, I'm getting even more value back than the burger I paid my money for. And then I, like, started thinking about money and stuff, and..."

She could feel the blood flowing into her skull. Her head was alive with thoughts about school, thoughts about her career, thoughts about her friends, her club activity, her family, and everything else on Earth. It made her lose sight of what was really important in her life.

"I just figured…if I knew what working for myself and earning money was like, then somehow—I don't know how, but somehow that'd help me build some experience in society. So, you know, I just kind of…"

Chiho's legs grew restless. Her voice ratcheted up in volume.

"I want to work so I can earn some money!"

"…Ah, I see." For some reason, Kisaki was grinning at her. "Not to change the subject, but do you know what you'd want to use the money for?"

"What for…? Um, well, if I can save up enough money, I'd like to get a nicer bow for myself. That and some arrows."

"Arrows? I don't know very much about *kyudo*, but are those arrows single-use or something?"

"No, not exactly, but sometimes they break or get all bent up during practice, so you have to keep buying more of them. It's a pretty expensive sport to get into in the first place, so I hate begging my parents for more money to keep it going, and plus, not all arrows are built the same way, so I figured if I had my own spending money, I could use it to find equipment that suited me a little better than the cheap stuff…"

The next few minutes evolved into a sort of newbie Q&A on *kyudo*, something that seemed less like a job interview and more like idle chatter at the coffee shop. The interview went on for about forty minutes all told.

"All right. Thanks a lot for stopping by today, Ms. Sasaki. I'll give you a call with my decision within two or three days."

"Certainly. Thank you very much for taking the time to see me."

Chiho stood up, bowed, and stepped toward the staff room door. She noticed her legs were quivering a little as she stepped outside.

"Oh, hello there." Maou, the employee who helped Chiho yesterday, nodded at her as he passed by. "I certainly wasn't expecting you to apply for a position the very next day!"

His smile was completely benign. He was practically welcoming her to the crew already.

"Oh, uh, thanks…"

But Chiho, drained of all tension now that the interview was over, could manage little more than a broken greeting.

"See you soon. Hope you get the job!"

She barely managed a bow in reply.

Her legs were still a little uneasy on the way out. Once the MgRonald was out of sight, she veered to one edge of the sidewalk and crouched down.

"I *so* blew it…"

"I want to earn money"? Seriously? That whole time, she kept blabbing on about all this extraneous nonsense instead of saying what actually needed to be said. Her mind was filled with regret. Being so frank about the salary aspect of it was so incredibly self-serving—it had to have made a terrible impression on that manager. She tried her best to be polite and upbeat, but in front of a real grown-up like that, she doubted she looked like much more than a teenager out of her comfort zone.

"Ugh… I'm gonna have to find somewhere else to hang out for a while…"

No way she had the guts to frequent a business that turned her down for a job. She'd have to suggest another stop to Kaori starting tomorrow. This, and many other negative thoughts, swirled around in her head as she staggered home in the darkening evening.

✳

Kisaki was in noticeably higher spirits after the teenaged job interviewee left the MgRonald by Hatagaya station.

"Marko?" she said to Maou, currently working the front counter.

"Yes?"

"I'm gonna have you train that girl just now."

"Whoa! You're hiring her already?"

"Yep. I wasn't expecting a lot 'cause her résumé was pretty much copied out of a book, but she's actually got a lot of spirit in her. I like that."

Kisaki was all smiles, but Maou winced at the mention of her documents.

"Geez, don't remind me about my interview…"

"Oh, I'll remind you all I want, Marko. You think I'm gonna forget someone who wrote 'I wanna eat good stuff' as their goal in their résumé?"

"Heh-heh…eesh." Maou was crestfallen but still curious about the new hire. She'd looked like just another girl when she passed him by. "But if her résumé didn't impress you, I guess the interview did?"

"Mm-hmm. I think we've got a student who'll actually stick to a constant shift schedule for a change. Try to go easy on her, okay?"

"Wow! I don't think you've told me to 'go easy' on anything."

Coming from her, this was high praise.

"Well," Kisaki explained, "she's a pretty serious girl, you know? Plus, the way she fielded my questions, there's no point being hard on her."

"Man, you really love her."

"Yep! Pretty much. She didn't try to fancy up her motives or anything. She kept it as straight as I do. So have fun with her starting tomorrow, okay?"

Kisaki turned around, practically humming to herself as she left. Maou groaned. "Geez," he mumbled to the cash register in front of him, "I only wrote that because I figured she'd kick me out if I wrote 'I want to conquer the world' in there…"

✳

"So how'd day two go?"

"Ugggh, I think my legs are gonna fall off…"

The full force of Chiho's groan came across loud and clear over the phone from her bedroom to Kaori. She had figured her legs and feet could put up with it, considering how much of a workout archery could be, but they were already impossibly sore. Her toes, her calves, her thighs, even her heels had fatigue draped over them in ways she never experienced before. She had given them a thorough massage in the bath, but they still didn't feel at all better.

"Yeah, I guess you're standing up the whole time, huh? Don't they give you any breaks?"

"Nope. My shifts haven't been long enough yet."

"Ohhh. You gotta work at least an eight-hour·shift, right?"

"Yeah, I think that was part of my first-day orientation…"

Apparently the law in Japan stated that high school students weren't allowed to work past ten in the evening. After discussing it, they agreed that she'd work no more than four hours on the weekdays, between school and the magic hour, and four to six hours on the weekends.

Chiho reflected on her first day as the conversation went on. After that disaster of an interview, she never thought she'd be hired in a million years.

Kisaki told her to fully clip her nails, so she took some extra time to take care of that before walking into the store, far more nervous than she was for the interview. The manager greeted her with a work contract and a uniform fitted for her size. It was designed for comfort, the chest area neither too tight nor too loose on her; she breathed a sigh of relief over that. When she looked into the staff room mirror after changing, the sight of herself in the MgRonald uniform she had seen a hundred times as a customer seemed incredibly out of place.

"All right," Kisaki said as she gave her a poke in the back. "To start out, we're gonna go around the restaurant so I can show you where everything is and what kind of work you'll be doing in each area. This isn't too large of a location, but there's a fair amount you'll need to remember…"

Kaori's words rang in Chiho's mind. For a moment, the image of getting yelled at for forgetting something made her anxious, but…

"There's no way you're going to remember it all on the first shot, so for now, just try to get a mental picture of what kind of work you'll generally be asked to do. You can take notes, too, if you like. That's gonna be your first job—learn all this stuff and get up to speed on how it all works around here."

"O-okay…"

"Right. First off, always wash your hands before going out into the dining space. I need to show you how, so let's hit the bathroom first."

They made the rounds, Kisaki guiding Chiho through the names of the assorted machines and work positions, the floor-map setup, and the work responsibilities at every area of the place. The memo paper she brought along with her was quickly filled to the brim with hastily written text. After all the times she stopped by here, there were still so many new names, new customs, and unfamiliar machines and areas to explore. It took an hour and a half just to go through the whole place. Between that and the subsequent training on things like how to greet customers, Chiho's first three hours as an employee passed by in a heartbeat.

"Hey, Marko?" Kisaki shouted at one of the crewmembers (calling the employees "crewmembers" was also something Chiho found novel about the place). Surprisingly, the call was answered by Maou, the crewmember who helped her out earlier.

"Oh, it's you!"

Apparently he remembered her. He removed his hat and gave her a warm smile.

"I, uh, today's my first job…I mean, my first day on the job! My name is Chiho Sasaki! It's great to be working with you!"

She stammered her way through her very first work introduction. Her face reddened with embarrassment, but Maou paid it no mind. "Sadao Maou," he said, the perfect picture of politeness. "Good to meet you, Ms. Sasaki."

Between his English ability and the way he carried himself, Chiho assumed he was quite a bit older than she—but face-to-face like this, he seemed surprisingly young. A student in college, maybe?

"I won't be here tomorrow, Sasaki, so he'll be taking care of you on your next shift." Kisaki placed a hand on Maou's shoulder. "He knows pretty much everything about this place, so go ahead and pepper him with all the questions you want."

"Wow, way to put the pressure on…" Maou flashed an uneasy smile and put his hat back on.

"Don't give her any wrong info, or else I'll make sure you pay for it, all right?"

Whether she was serious about it or not, the words had an obvious effect on Maou's demeanor. He chuckled nervously.

"No problem, boss. This is nothing compared to leading an army of half a million."

"Huh?"

Chiho raised an eyebrow. *Half a million?*

Kisaki shrugged. "If it wasn't for his tendency to lapse into grandiose metaphors like that, I'd have no complaints with Marko."

It didn't sound all that grandiose to Chiho. Just odd.

"Heh-heh... Really, though, Sasaki, if you think you'll want to work here a while, don't be afraid to ask me, or Ms. Kisaki, or anybody else around here if you have any questions. If you don't remember it the first time—or the second time, for that matter—then please, just ask again. Nobody on the crew's gonna yell at you for forgetting something."

"A-all right..."

"Yeah, and if someone does, tell me about it, okay? Because if they do"—Kisaki's face took on a suddenly twisted, demonic snarl—"I'll show them hell itself."

"Agh!" Chiho couldn't help but yelp at the half-crazed smile.

"If I can translate for Ms. Kisaki," Maou said in a half chuckle, "if you're going to disappoint a customer after messing something up because you winged it and got it wrong, it's a lot better for everyone to take the time to ask someone instead. So really, don't be afraid to bother anyone. That's how all of us learned how to do our jobs, so pretty much everyone should be able to answer your questions."

"...Okay. I'll try my best to."

She had already experienced the credo Kisaki and Maou brought to their work as a customer. If that was how they put it, the rest of the crew must be equally as talented. And even with how nice they were to her, Chiho resolved to work as hard as she could to not be too much of a drag on them.

*　*　*

"Oh, maaaan. You sure you didn't die and go to heaven or something?" Kaori, listening to the story, sounded supremely jealous over the phone. "'Cause, like, whenever I asked a question, it was always like 'Didn't someone show it to you already?'"

"Ha-ha-ha…"

"So if that was yesterday, what was today like?"

"Well…"

Day one, after the intros, was pretty much nothing but studying. Today, on her second day, she was finally assigned something resembling work.

"I still didn't get to cook or anything, but I spent the whole shift on cleaning duty, pretty much."

"Cleaning duty?"

"Uh-huh. I wiped up all the trays with this disinfected cloth, and then I wiped down the tables so I could learn all the numbers associated with them. After that, I restocked the shelves with stuff like napkins and straws and to-go bags from storage. I had to clean those shelves, too…"

"Did you take out the garbage and stuff, too?"

"No, they didn't let me do that yet."

"No?"

"Yeah. They're, like, superstrict on separating all the garbage, so I gotta learn how all that works. Plus, you know how the Mag's garbage area's near the entrance, right? I still haven't learned how to guide customers around and answer their questions, so that's probably not gonna happen for a little while."

"…Wow, the grass really is greener, huh?"

"Maybe, but…oooh, staying on my feet for four hours in a row is just killing me. And you were right, Kao—this one customer asked me, like, this impossible question. I had this huge IN TRAINING button on and everything."

"Ooh, that fast, huh? How'd it go?"

"Well, that Maou crewmember was with me pretty much the

whole time except when we were really busy, so he handled the whole thing."

"*Can I, like, have your job, Sasachi?*" Kaori sounded fairly serious about the offer. "*'Cause it sounds really great. I wanna see you in action sometime! I promise I won't embarrass you like Yoshiya will, too.*"

"...Go easy on me, okay?"

After the conversation meandered elsewhere and Chiho hung up the phone, she recalled the "impossible question" she was asked. It came from a man in his fifties or so, asking if the Hatagaya MgRonald location had any birthday cakes. She had never heard of it. Why would a burger joint be selling cakes? Nobody told her about that so far.

She was about to give that answer when Maou intervened. "I apologize, sir," he said, "but this location doesn't accept reservations for birthday parties, so I'm afraid we don't have any cakes in stock."

The quick explanation made Chiho's eyes prick upward. She had never connected MgRonald with birthday parties before. The thought had never even occurred to her.

"Within central Tokyo," Maou continued next to the deer-in-headlights Chiho, "there's one location in Meguro and one in Suginami that accept party reservations. The Suginami restaurant is gonna be the closer one, since it's on the Keio rail line. Let me grab you the phone number real quick."

With that, Maou darted off to the staff room and came back with an ad circular Chiho had never seen before. She stared blankly at the customer as he left.

"That's not something we see mentioned too often," Maou said, showing her another copy of the circular, "but yeah, you can make reservations for birthday parties at some locations. Mostly the suburban ones, though, since our inner-city MgRonalds are usually on the small side."

The circular included a picture of a boy, perhaps kindergarten age, enjoying a party—balloons, the whole bit—with a MgRonald crewmember supervising.

"Young kids, you know, they look up to people who work at places they go to all the time. Some of 'em really like the uniform and our hats and so on. That's a pretty rare request, though, so don't worry about it too much."

"…"

Chiho cursed her thoughtlessness as she read through the circular. If that was the question the middle-aged man had for her, chances were he'd intended to hold a party for his grandson or something. If she had gone ahead and given him the wrong information, the whole thing might've been called off.

"…Guess that's why I better ask if I don't know, huh?"

"Hmm?"

"Like, I had never heard of that before, so I just assumed it didn't exist…"

"Ohh. Yeah, well, I've never seen it myself, either, so…"

"Sorry about that. I'll try to be more careful."

"It's cool." Maou nodded. "Don't let it get you too down, all right? Just keep it in mind, and you're guaranteed not to make that same mistake again."

"…All right."

"Oh, but don't expect that everything's gonna go perfect from now on, either."

"Huh?"

"Well, I mean, if you did everything perfectly during your training period, there's not much point in me being around, y'know? Me and Ms. Kisaki and everyone else on the crew had to go through the same thing, so really, making mistakes is kinda part of the job description when you're starting out. As long as you learn from them, it's all good."

The advice, given freely but with ample consideration for Chiho's feelings, helped her feel a little more at ease. It certainly wasn't a matter of Maou going easy on her.

"Sure," Chiho replied, "I'll try not to rely on you guys too much, though. I don't want to be embarrassed to get paid for this."

Maou's eyebrows arched up a little at this unexpected self-admonition. "Huh," he said. "I think I'm starting to see why Ms. Kisaki said you'd probably stick around for a while."

"Oh?" a quizzical Chiho asked. She didn't know why, but if the manager apparently had high hopes for her, that certainly couldn't be a bad thing. Little by little, she was using her eyes, her ears, her whole body, to understand the environment around her. This, she supposed, was what work was. And as she reflected on this in bed, her eyes grew heavier and heavier.

"...Better go brush my teeth," she said to herself, almost dropping her phone as she worked her creaky legs out of bed and to the bathroom.

✳

Chiho's adventures in part-time employment continued over the ensuing two weeks. She wasn't at MgRonald every day, but by the end of her seventh shift, she was starting to feel she was past the initial hump, at least. It was tiring work, and not every moment of it was fun, but picturing her next shift was never a depressing thought for her.

"Yeah, so why're you acting all gloomy, huh?"

Kaori had a point. Despite her generally glowing review of shift life at MgRonald, there was still a dark shadow covering her face.

"Well...I like the manager and all the people on the crew, but...I guess that's kind of the problem, actually."

"What do you mean?"

"Um...I think I might be gaining weight."

"Huh?"

Beyond her first orientation session, Chiho had been ordered to eat something from MgRonald's regular menu for dinner on each of her six subsequent shifts. She was a fan, of course, and getting a free meal out of work was nothing to sniff at—but all the calories were starting to become a concern.

"I'm glad they're feeding you and all, but every time? That's kind of rough. Why're they doing that to you?"

"I guess their reasoning is that I can't give recommendations to customers unless I know how things taste for myself. I know we've been there a lot, but there's a ton of stuff on the menu I've never eaten before..."

"Ohhh." Kaori nodded. This made sense to her. "Yeah, I've never been there for breakfast, I guess. That, and I never really bother with stuff that's not on the value menu, huh?"

"Yeah," Chiho replied, trying not to make it sound like she was bragging about her job too much. "But once my training's over, I'll have to start paying for my own meals. I think I still get thirty percent off or something, though."

"Ooh, nice." Kaori let out a jealous sigh. "You really lucked out with that job! Everyone's really nice, they aren't pushing a lot of crap on you, and they even let you eat for free! Man, I bet I coulda stayed on a while longer over there. So what do you think, though? Has it helped you figure out life as a high school grad yet?"

"Not...really, no."

She had almost forgotten about that thorny issue—the very one that had inspired her to seek a job in the first place. She was happy enough with the work, but the whole point behind it—her quest to figure out how she wanted to proceed with life in a couple of years—was still an open question. She'd need to submit that survey form pretty soon, and the teacher conferences at the end of the month were just a few days away.

"Hey, uh, Sasaki?" Yoshiya pitched in. "How much are you makin' an hour?"

"How much? Um, it's eight hundred yen an hour while I'm in training; that's what they pay high school students. Once it's over I think it'll go up by fifty yen."

Beyond that, apparently, it would depend on her performance. As Kisaki put it, Maou was a living legend around the MgRonald location thanks to his earning a hundred-yen raise after two months—in orders, just one month out of his training period. The dedication he brought to the job was obvious in Chiho's mind. It'd take a while, she reasoned, before she could reach that level of talent.

"Damn, so if you work six hours a day, you'll make, like, almost five thousand? Wooooow."

"Yeah, *if* she does," Kaori snapped back. "Yoshiya, could you stop being amazed at Sasachi's fast-food job and worry about your career guidance survey a little more? You know how strict your parents are with you."

Chiho had first met Kaori upon entering this high school, but Kaori and Yoshiya had apparently known each other since their elementary years. Every now and then, she'd bring up little clues to their past like this. Kaori's acerbic criticism when dealing with Yoshiya was something honed across years of interaction, but given how well they got along with each other anyway, Chiho assumed neither of them took things too personally.

This time, however, Yoshiya's reaction drifted from the norm.

"Ah, I dunno about…strict, exactly. Like, nowadays, it's like I'm not even part of their lives anymore. I'm not even kidding when I say that I don't think they'll show up for the conference."

"Oh?" asked Koari.

"What do you mean, Yoshiya?" Chiho added.

"Well, you know about my brothers, right, Shoji?"

"Ohhh." Kaori sagely nodded.

"Wait, you've got brothers, Kohmura?" Chiho inquired.

In the two years that Chiho had known Yoshiya, it was the first time she had heard of this. It naturally struck her curiosity, but Yoshiya winced at the topic, something he seemed to not want to bring up.

"Mmm, I was hoping Sasaki wouldn't have to know about it…"

"Huh? Why not?"

"Ah, 'cause if you knew about them, I figured you'd make fun of me for—*ow!*"

Kaori's pencil case, packed to the gills with writing instruments, made a clean hit on Yoshiya's face. It whizzed right past Chiho's ear along the way. She could tell there was a lot of heft to it.

"Well, that's why we treat you like an idiot!" Kaori shouted. "Because of that attitude! You know Sasachi isn't like that!"

"...Geez, the zipper bounced right off my teeth..."

"Well, go wash my case down and disinfect it! Right now!"

"I totally can't believe you, Shoji..."

"Whoa! Guys, calm down!"

Chiho wound up having to listen to them bicker over her head for the next five minutes. Yoshiya still didn't want to talk about his siblings, so Kaori took the reins for him.

"So, like, Yoshiya has two older brothers, but get this—the oldest one's a judge, and the other one's a doctor, right?"

"What?!" Chiho couldn't help but shout. This was beyond anything she expected.

Yoshiya, for his part, glumly shook his head. "Quit making up stuff, Shoji," he said. "The oldest one wants to be a judge, but he's still in his legal apprenticeship. And my other brother's taking the test for his medical license this year, so he's not a doctor yet."

"Right, that," Kaori agreed. "And meanwhile, the youngest kid's failing out of Sasahata North, and you can kinda see how that makes things awkward around the dinner table, right?"

"Geez, don't spell it out like that," Yoshiya groaned. "I mean, my parents kept pressing me to work really hard like both of my brothers did, but I think they've, like, given up on that. They barely even talk to me anymore—I told them about that mock exam and they were just like 'Oh? Hmm.' And it's not like I got some kind of other special talent, either. Basically, I'm just waitin' until I can get the hell outta there."

"Kohmura..."

"That's why I was thinking," he went on. "You 'n' Shoji, you both got work experience, right? Maybe I could find a part-time job somewhere so I can get out sooner."

Chiho didn't pursue the subject any further—Yoshiya looked peeved enough revealing what little he did about his family—but to her, the kid seemed like he could be in some serious trouble.

Kaori must have felt the same way. "Yoshiya," she said, her voice low and serious, "if you start working as it is now, it's gonna go beyond repeating a year. You'd pretty much be forced to drop out."

"Well," Yoshiya replied, "as long as I'm making money, it's all good, isn't it? Y'know how people say the stuff you study in school doesn't even help out in college at all these days. That's what I'm probably gonna write in my survey, I guess. Go straight to work, 'n' all."

He was back to his usual free-wheeling tone. Chiho couldn't tell how serious he was being.

*

"Hey there." Kisaki struck up a conversation with Chiho, who was currently manning the register. "Something got you down? Did you have a question about something?"

"Oh! Hello. Um, nothing like that, but…well, maybe it is, actually."

"Hmm?"

Her head was occupied with thoughts about her future and the conversation she'd had at school earlier. Yoshiya, Kaori, and herself were all trying to squint into the future, trying to figure out which path was the right one for each of them, and all completely failing to reach a conclusion.

"So I got to talking to my friends at school about the future, but… I really don't know what I should do yet, and I'm gonna have to talk about it at a parent-teacher conference in a few days. I have to think of *something*, but… I dunno."

"Oh, that kind of thing?" Kisaki nodded, her face showing her concern.

"Yeah… Sorry I'm not too focused on—"

"Well, I can give you a grown-up's advice, or some completely irresponsible advice. Which do you want to hear first?"

"Huh?" Chiho exclaimed. She was expecting a verbal warning not to space out on the clock—but not only was Kisaki empathizing with her, she was bringing the conversation down an exceedingly odd direction.

"...Okay, how about the grown-up advice?"

"Sure. From a grown-up's perspective, what you tell your teacher or guidance counselor about your future means absolute jack squat, so there's no point worrying about it at all."

"Huh?!"

This felt outrageous to Chiho. It sounded like just another grown-up giving her half-baked advice that did nothing to help her. But, judging by her facial expression, Kisaki was expecting that reaction.

"Why do you think that is?" she asked. "Well, it's because the grown-ups asking you that question already had it resolved for themselves ages ago."

"Wh-what do you mean...?"

"Once you're old enough, it gets a lot easier to look back at your high school years and see what you could've done to be more successful later on. That's why they don't understand why kids like you are getting so worried about this crossroads in their lives—they went down that path long ago. And most grown-ups, you know—they're kind of embarrassed about how they acted in high school. They had more passion than intelligence, and they were totally honest with themselves back then. So that's why outside of your parents, your teachers, and whoever you're working with at the test-prep center or whatever, you should just ignore advice from anyone who doesn't know anything about you."

"The test-prep center?"

"Sure. It's their whole job to make sure you can have a smooth transition to wherever it is you're going. When it comes to thinking about their students, at least, I think you can trust them."

"I see..."

"Now, for the totally irresponsible advice: Most worries about career guidance pretty much boil down to 'I don't know what I should do, what I should aim for, what I should study.' You don't know what kind of work clicks with you. You don't know what you should pick as your major in college."

"Right. Exactly. So—"

"If I wanted to be totally impartial here, I'd say you go to a low-tuition public university, take law or premed, and become a doctor or judge or whatever. It's getting hard for lawyers to keep their heads above water these days, even, so I'd say public service would be the way to go."

"But..." Chiho hesitated at the eerily familiar advice.

"But," Kisaki continued with a sly smile, "me telling you that doesn't really help you decide on anything, does it?"

"No..."

"So in that case, why bother thinking that far ahead in the first place? After all, who can even say where you'll be this time next year? Because there ain't a grown-up in the world who knows that for themselves, and yet they're asking kids like you to make this huge, vague life decision. It's really sad, what they make you do."

Kisaki's voice grew to a crescendo.

"The whole career guidance thing is about thinking about what you'll do today for the sake of tomorrow. Because maybe you don't know where you'll be next year, but you got a pretty good idea of what you want to do tomorrow, right?"

"Tomorrow, huh...?"

"Yeah. It's literally that. Today, and tomorrow, just like it is on the calendar. Your career's in the future, and what's the future besides a whole long succession of todays and tomorrows, anyway? Most people out there...they aren't intelligent enough to look past everything in front of them and seriously think about life one or two years down the line. Instead of that, you gotta work with what you have. Reach out to tomorrow—reach out to what you can still grasp with one hand—and you'll be grasping next year before you even know it."

"Just to tomorrow..."

"Right. So!"

Suddenly, Kisaki put a hand on Chiho's head. She looked up in response.

"Now that I've clouded up your mind even more like the grown-up

I am, how about we focus on the work we've got right now? Like I said, what you do today has everything to do with how tomorrow works out."

"Oh! Um, okay."

"You gotta keep a clear mind when you're handling money. Make sure you're telling your five-thousand-yen bills from the ten-thousand-yen ones."

"S-sure thing!"

Chiho went back to work, although the cloud wasn't fully extinguished from her mind. On no less than two occasions today, her lack of focus caused her to almost treat five-thousand-yen banknotes like they were ten-thousand-yen bills. If it wasn't for the rule that change for high-denomination bills had to be counted with another crewmember as a witness, she would've quite literally given away her day's salary to her customers.

"I apologize. I'm gonna focus on my work now."

This time around, she felt she really meant that from the heart. The fog hadn't lifted from her head, but she still felt a great deal relieved compared to before.

"Perfect," Kisaki replied. "Now I'm glad I gave you all that self-important junk a second ago. I gotta head over to the office for a little while, but if you run into any problems, ask another crewmember, all right?"

"Okay!"

"Good luck, Chi."

"Sure!"

The slightly contrived encouragement Kisaki gave her as she waved and disappeared behind the staff room door didn't sink in for a moment. Then:

"…Wait, did she call me 'Chi'?"

Her next visit to the staff room came at the end of the shift. There, she was surprised to find Maou in street clothes.

"Oh, you gettin' off, too, Sasaki?"

"Yeah, thanks. Are you done, too?"

"Uh-huh. Bit earlier than usual. I was here since morning today."

The Hatagaya MgRonald was not a twenty-four-hour location. It closed at midnight, with the closing of the rail line for the day, and while Maou usually stuck around after Chiho's departure in order to handle closing duty, his early arrival today apparently meant he was going home sooner as well.

But Chiho's concern was elsewhere.

"Um…Maou?"

"Hmm?"

"Are, are you going home like that?"

"Yeah…?"

The curt reply left Chiho speechless. It was spring, but the nights still dipped into near-freezing—and his thin, long-sleeved shirt and hoodie weren't near enough protection against the cold.

"Aren't you, um, cold at all?"

"Well, yeah, but I couldn't get any of my laundry dry this morning, y'know?"

She was rendered speechless again.

"All the Laundromats around here raised their prices a bit ago, so I've tried doing the laundry by hand lately…but you know how winter clothes are, right? I didn't think it'd take *that* long for them to dry."

It was the first time Maou spoke of his private life to Chiho. It offered perhaps too candid a look for her tastes, but over the past few days, she had gotten used to Maou giving her little glimpses of his life like this.

"I figure it's gonna take two days to get everything dry," he continued, "so…you know, gotta wear something, right?"

Chiho didn't think drying times were the issue here, but she didn't want to add further insult to Maou's laundry-related injury. "Yeah, you're right," she said. "I guess you could probably deal with it better than I could for a day or two. It's about to get warmer anyway."

She removed her hat, preparing to change out of her uniform.

"Oh, is it gonna get warmer?"

Then she turned back around.

"Um… Well, yeah, it's April, so…pretty much right at the middle of spring."

"Ohhh. Okay. That's how it works, huh? First winter, then spring. Right. Guess *that's* not any different."

"Um, Maou?"

Chiho stared at him, this grown man marveling at what seemed to be a great, reassuring discovery to him. Maou couldn't help but notice.

"……I knew that."

"……Right."

With an awkward good-bye, Maou stepped out of the staff room. But after she finished changing and said her good-byes to the remaining crew on duty, she discovered Maou outside the restaurant, standing in the middle of the sidewalk.

"Maou? Were you waiting for something?"

"Dahh…"

"Oh! It's raining…"

The reason for Maou's distress was fairly obvious. Chiho doubted he had an umbrella with him.

"That's always how it is, too, isn't it?" Maou lamented. "The one day you need an umbrella, and you never have one on hand…"

"Oh, um," Chiho said, taking a compact umbrella from her bag. "The weather report this morning said it was gonna rain all night, though…"

"Oh, I don't have a TV."

Another rather surprising revelation. Today was proving to be full of them.

"You don't…?"

"Well, guess I'll have to run all the way home. Hope my laundry's all dry by now…" Maou lifted up the hood on his sweatshirt and took a deep breath. "Be careful on your way home, Sasa—"

"…Um!" Chiho found herself proclaiming as she searched her

mind for a way to keep Maou from jogging off. "Where do you live, Maou?!"

"Where? Uh, more toward Sasazuka station…"

"I'm going that way, too! You wanna share an umbrella with me?!"

"Hey, thanks a lot for doing this."

"Oh, not at all, um… You're welcome," Chiho whispered in response to Maou's carefree gratitude. The offer had come all too casually, but it was actually the first time she had shared an umbrella with a man in her life. The only silver lining was that the umbrella she carried in her *kyudo* bag was larger than usual for the fold-up variety, so she didn't need to make that much physical contact with him.

"Oh, but your shoulder…"

However, it was the taller Maou who wound up carrying it. He held it at an angle the whole time to keep Chiho dry, resulting in most of his opposite shoulder getting soaked along the way.

"Ah, it's fine," Maou chirped in reply. "It beats getting all-the-way wet, at least. But, hey, is it gonna be raining a lot like this from now on?"

"Huh? Um, it's hard to say… Probably, though."

"Really? Hmm… That's sure a drag. Now it'll be even harder to keep the laundry dry, huh?"

"Well, it'll be warmer soon, though. You could probably buy a washing machine for pretty cheap, too."

"A *what*?" The surprise was written across Maou's face. "Oh, no way. I don't have near enough room for two of those huge things. Plus, they gotta cost, like, a ton, right?"

"Um? Yeah, uh…I guess?"

Chiho hesitated for a moment, worried that she made too many assumptions about Maou's financial situation. Then another question popped up in her head.

Two of them?

"I mean," he continued, "maybe they don't look that big in the

Laundromat, but even if I could get a washer and dryer unit up there, they'd wind up blocking the corridor in my apartment anyway."

"Uhm…uh, Maou, I'm not talking about some big commercial thing. I mean a regular home washer."

"Huh?"

"Huh?"

"…A home washer?"

"Yeah…"

Did Maou think the only washing machines in the world were the giant cubes at the Laundromat?

"I mean, at the store and so on, they sell washers that aren't too much bigger than the trash containers at MgRonald. They're fully automatic and everything, and if you're on a tight budget, you could get a dual-compartment one for pretty cheap…"

"…Seriously?"

"Seriously."

Chiho, indeed, was starting to wonder if Maou was being serious. Maou acted like all of this was a complete shock to him.

"If you're in an apartment building, there's probably a water linkup somewhere in the hallway. I think you could install the machine next to that…"

"Oh! Yeah!" Maou beamed with delight. "There is! That was for a washing machine?! 'Cause I was using it to fill a bucket with water and do the laundry in that!"

"…Well, at least you were using it for laundry."

"But…wow." Maou repeatedly nodded to himself. "You could buy your own washers… I thought it was a monopoly run by a launderers' guild or something."

This was thoroughly confusing Chiho. He was a completely different person from the MgRonald crewmember she thought she knew. But watching him, eyes a-twinkle as he legitimately appeared to be making a new discovery in life, was almost cute, in a way.

"Hey, can I ask one more question?"

"Um, sure, what is it?"

"So it's gonna get warmer and rainier, right? That's probably gonna make my vegetables rot even if I keep 'em in the shade, won't it? How do you handle that, Sasaki?"

Chiho's eyes virtually unscrewed themselves from their sockets. *This* was even crazier.

"The *shade*?!" she exclaimed. "Just put them in the refrigerator, and..." She didn't bother finishing the sentence. She knew what Maou was going to say in two seconds' time anyway.

"I don't have one of those."

"Oh, you should really buy one! I mean, maybe you can handle the laundry yourself, but you're gonna be in big trouble if you don't even have a fridge! If your food keeps going bad on you, you're gonna get really sick!"

"...Oh. You think so?"

"You know how in the past few years, it's been a pretty mild spring and then it goes right into this superhot summer, right? Veggies and stuff start going off on you practically the moment you buy them!"

"Wow, really? Go off on you? What, do they grow legs or something?"

"It's just an expression! And what do you mean, 'Wow, really'? It was the same thing last year and the year before! If you leave raw food out in the summertime, it'll go bad!"

"O-okay! Okay! I was thinking that I wanted a fridge, too, actually, so I'll buy it, okay? ...Oh, and..."

"And?"

"...Where do you think I could buy a washer and refrigerator for cheap?"

"..."

This didn't appear to be an act. From the changes in seasons to the existence of discount appliance stores, Maou really did seem to lack any semblance of common sense. And he was such a star at work, too... Chiho wasn't sure whether discovering this gap in his personality was something to be delighted or annoyed about.

"Listen, Maou, were you, like, raised somewhere outside Japan or something? You speak English really well and stuff, so… Did you come home from a stint overseas?"

The idea made sense to her. All that fluency, combined with all that bemused befuddlement about modern Japanese life, suggested that he was living somewhere overseas until fairly recently. But:

"No, not exactly like that. Not 'coming home,' per se. That, and I learned English 'cause I thought it'd be useful for my work."

He makes "learning" it sound so easy, Chiho thought. She decided to steer the conversation back to its original purpose. Prying too much ran the risk of offending Maou, and something told her that too much prying would lead to even more questions anyway.

"Well, if you need appliances, I think the Socket City by Shinju-ku's west exit has a lot of cheap stuff. You could also look at the Donkey OK Discount Store in Hounancho… That's the place with all the bicycles on sale in front."

Maou nodded at her, eyes open wide. "Oh, I know those! I just thought all the big stores would have nothing but really fancy expensive stuff."

"Oh, well, Donkey OK's actually more about really cheap stuff, you know? Like, if you aren't too picky, you could get a bike there for a few thousand yen."

"Whoa! A few thousand? You sure know a lot about this stuff, Sasaki…"

It was as if Chiho had just revealed the meaning of life to Maou. He was mesmerized. Chiho was about to comment on this before Maou stopped her.

"No wonder Ms. Kisaki's given you that nickname so quickly!"

"Huh?"

"She started calling you 'Chi,' you know?"

Chiho's heart skipped a beat. "Y-yes, I do…?"

"I heard about that, too. Everybody did. I'm willing to bet you'll be Chi to the whole crew starting tomorrow. That's the way Ms. Kisaki works—once she gives you a nickname, that pretty much means you've graduated from training. Like, you aren't officially done until you're on the crew for a month, but if you got a nickname *this* fast, you'll probably get that bump in your hourly wage a little earlier than what she originally told you."

"What? R-really?" Chiho blinked in surprise, unsure how nicknames were connected to her salary.

"Uh-huh. None of us really know why, but there's kind of this unwritten rule that once Ms. Kisaki starts calling a new hire by some nickname or another, that means he or she's a full-fledged part of the crew now."

Kaori's past experiences flashed across Chiho's mind again. Was the whole "training period" thing just a façade, then? Would people start yelling at her if she couldn't do all the work by herself?

"Oh," continued Maou, probably not aware of her concerns, "but it's not like you're going to be fed to the sharks or anything, so don't worry about that. I'm still gonna be with you until you can be fully independent."

"Oh! Thank you."

She appreciated the reassurance, even if the way he promised he was "still gonna be with" her made her a little embarrassed.

"Either way, though, Ms. Kisaki's definitely indicating to us that you deserve to be treated like the rest of us on the job, Sasaki. Keep up the good work, okay? No need to feel like you're under pressure or whatever."

"Um, okay...!"

The two fell silent for a moment or two, Chiho having trouble looking Maou in the face.

"My place is over this way. What about you, Sasaki?"

"Oh, I'm across the street...but I can accompany you if you want!"

Abandoning Maou at this point would soak him before he reached his front door.

"No, no, that's okay," he replied. "I wouldn't want you getting in trouble on the way back or anything."

"But..."

Chiho tried to resist, but Maou just smiled and turned toward a nearby mailbox. "You see that?" he said, beaming. "I got an umbrella of my own now. Thanks a lot for taking me all the way here, though. I appreciate it."

In his hand was a shoddy plastic umbrella, the tip rusted and the ribs already bent out of shape before he even opened it up. Someone must have hung it on the mailbox and promptly forgotten about it. It had been abandoned for a while, and a fairly decent amount of rainwater had accumulated inside it. But Maou cheerfully handed Chiho her own umbrella back and opened up his new find.

"Perfect," he said, nodding his satisfaction. "Thanks again! Take care on the way home. Oh, and…"

"Hmm?"

"I hope this doesn't sound weird or anything…"

"Umm, what?"

Maou hesitated for a bit, letting out a self-conscious cough.

"Keep up the good work tomorrow, Chi."

"…?!"

"Anyway, see you at the next shift."

"Um, y-yeah. Of course. Sleep well."

It was a completely unexpected attack.

Chiho watched as he waved and went on his way, then brought a hand to her cheek. She couldn't have guessed the last time a man called her by a cutesy nickname. In fact, before Kisaki came out with it, she had completely forgot that "Chi" was what people called her as a young child. And now people much more talented than her, much more grown-up than her, were using it…

"…!"

She gasped a little. The shoulder she was rubbing against Maou under the umbrella a few moments ago seemed warm to the touch.

Her cousin, the one she'd looked up to as a grade schooler, was now a husband and a father. For as long as she could remember, he always seemed so incredibly mature in her eyes. He taught her all about things she'd never known before, much like Maou was now. And now, for some reason, the two of them were overlapping with each other in her imagination.

Someone who's reliable, who knows a lot of mysterious things, who's really grown-up...but who's also got a screw or two loose...

"Huh? I... Huh?"

Now Chiho's face was getting warm. She had difficulty turning away from the path Maou walked down for a little while.

✳

"Wow, they don't look alike at all..."

Unable to help herself, Chiho broke out the photo album from her cousin's wedding once she was back home. He looked absolutely nothing like Maou. Maybe this was a little rude to her cousin, but Maou was way, way cooler than...

"Ugh, what am I thinking?! ...Ow!"

She tried snapping the book shut so quickly that one of her fingers got caught between the pages. It ached for the rest of the night. She returned the album to her puzzled mother and glared at her black-and-blue fingertip as she went to her room.

Flinging herself lifelessly into bed, she lay facedown, buried her head in a pillow, and sighed, legs flailing in the air.

"...What is *with* me?"

She began pumping her legs more and more rapidly. The bedsprings began to creak.

"Oww!!"

The pumping motion caused her body to drift across the bed, causing her to inadvertently smash the toes of one foot against the wall. She shot back up, grabbing her foot as she teared up a little.

"What am I even doing... Huh?"

Just as she was regretting her bizarre behavior, she heard her phone vibrate. It was a new text. She tried to keep her weight off her sore toenails as she picked it up off her desk.

"Oh, Kohmura?"

The text was short and to the point:

<Me and shoji're eating at the mag 2moro>

"Noooo…"

Without a moment's hesitation, she replied. "'Don't, I'm not ready yet'… There."

Kisaki and Maou were impressed with her, apparently, but to be honest, she had no idea what they saw in her. She knew her friends or family would stop by sooner or later, but *tomorrow*? That was just the *worst* timing. She knew she'd get so worked up over it that she'd immediately screw something up. Something big.

As she fretted over that, another text appeared.

"Huh? From Kao?"

She read it aloud: "<Yoshiya just texted me that we're going to your job tomorrow. Why'd you tell him? He wouldn't know you had a shift tomorrow otherwise.> …Oh."

Chiho cursed her careless mistake. Tomorrow would be the first Sunday shift she ever had. Before now, she had never been in MgRonald for more than four hours at once. There was no way to avoid an encounter, no matter how much she begged him to stay home.

"Oh, man… What'll I do when they show up…?"

They were her friends, of course, but among the rest of the crew and the other customers, she knew she'd have to treat them like anyone else. But she had seen this kind of scene in dramas before: someone's friend shows up, and the hapless victim's coworkers reveal all these hidden secrets to them like it was their God-given right…

"Ahh," she said to herself, "that only happens in, like, bars or other family places. That couldn't happen someplace like MgRonald, could it?"

If her mother or father stopped by, that was another thing. A tad embarrassing, maybe, but her mother had every right to check up on her daughter via Kisaki and her other coworkers. But her school friends were different. Try as she did, she just couldn't imagine how the situation would turn out.

Then she had an idea.

"Hey! Maybe I could ask Maou…"

She reached out for her phone, but:

"…Oh, I don't have his number…"

Maou was practically her shadow for the entirety of the training period, but they had never exchanged addresses or phone numbers. She had no way of contacting him, and besides:

"Wh-why did I think about asking Maou? I could ask a million other people…"

For some reason, until the moment she realized she didn't have his number, she never thought for a moment about contacting anyone except Maou. It didn't seem like something to contact the location's general phone line about—asking something like "My friends are coming tomorrow; how should I handle them?" seemed incredibly immature to her.

"It's not like they're guaranteed to show up," she reassured herself. "Maybe I could ask someone in tomorrow's shift for some advice. Someone like…"

She took a look at the shift schedule she had inserted in her notebook. Then she remembered that it consisted of two sheets.

"Oh…phone numbers."

The second one was a list of crewmember contacts. It allowed people to contact Kisaki in case of emergency or other people in case they wanted to swap shifts. She had received that sheet as part of her first-day packet. Her own number wasn't on there yet, but Maou's was.

What kind of place does Maou live in, anyway? No TV, no washer, no refrigerator… Nothing too luxurious, probably. But given how the schedule showed him working the afternoon–evening shift almost daily, he couldn't have been a college student. Maybe an actor or musician, chasing his dreams in the big city…?

"No!" Chiho said. "That's not what I want to know! I just want to know if it's okay to chat with my friends a little if they show up, and stuff…"

Between the way he acted and how hard he worked, Maou seemed like a solid enough guy. Nothing lurking behind the scenes. Maybe he was taking correspondence courses or something? So he could get into college or vo-tech?

"I *said*, that's not what I want to know!"

He must have been pretty poor, living alone in an apartment, but it seemed like he had his life under control. Between his hair, his bag, and his clothing, he looked perfectly fine (if not exactly on the cutting edge of fashion), and his uniform was always clean and neatly washed. Perhaps he had a significant other of some sort taking care of his personal life?

"…!"

Why am I imagining stuff like that? I hate this. But I don't even know why I hate this. But, in terms of common sense, it was totally possible. *But so what if Maou has a GF or whatever? It's got nothing to do with me…*

"No! No, no, no! No *way* he's got one!"

"Chiho! What are you hollering about?!"

The sound of her mother yelling from downstairs made Chiho blush.

Actually, why not ask…her? Talking over the phone was too much of a hurdle right now. She didn't want people to think she was some frivolous girl, bothering them with stupid questions late at night.

"…No. I don't."

Chiho put the schedule away with her notebook, turned out the light in her room, and went downstairs to talk things over. But the moment things went dark, a corner of her head was flooded with images of the imaginary life partner next to Maou: *Some brave, gallant housewife, maybe, supporting his busy work schedule at home? Or maybe he got saddled with some lazy woman who wastes all his money? Or maybe someone who goes around in kimonos every day? Opposites attract, as they say, after all… Or maybe a woman who has it all together, working on her career just like Maou is?*

"Oh, it doesn't matter, though. It doesn't matter!"

It was freaking her out, her mind creating all these concrete images of Maou's girlfriend. She shook her head to cast them all away.

"What doesn't matter?"

Chiho's mother heard her talking to herself down the stairs.

"Oh, nothing," she replied as she moved on to the living room. "Listen, though, I wanted to ask you something…"

"Sure," her mother said as Chiho settled down on the sofa. "But are you still worried about that career-counseling thing? What happened with that in the end?"

"…Agh!" she yelped. She had totally forgotten. That was due next Monday.

✳

After the rest of the evening spent staring at the career survey, the only things Chiho could fill out on it were her name and classroom number. It was still giving her a headache by the time she departed for work the following day, but she had a bigger and more immediate issue to deal with—whether Yoshiya would actually show or not.

Kaori had texted the previous night that she'd "try to slow him down so he doesn't do anything too stupid," but even with that reassurance, there was something superawkward about being seen at her part-time job. Now she knew exactly why Kaori didn't tell her about *her* job until she quit. It wasn't for any logical reason; dealing with them in a different situation from the norm just didn't feel right.

Chiho had discussed the issue with her mother the previous night, of course. "Well," she suggested, "as long as it doesn't affect your work much, I'm sure they'll let you guys chat for a bit, won't they? Just make sure your manager and coworkers don't start glaring at you."

It wasn't very effective advice. She didn't know why, but Kisaki apparently had high praise for her. She didn't want that praise to fly out the window because of something she did.

So, in the end:

"Hey, um… I think my friends might pay me a visit during this shift…"

She kept her promise. If she didn't understand something, she was supposed to ask a fellow crewmember. So she asked Maou.

"Your friends? From school?"

"Y-yeah. But if they show up, though…"

Halfway through the question, Chiho began to feel incredibly silly. Surely this was something she was capable of handling by herself. These weren't strangers, after all. Just work through it, and everything will be fine. No?

As if to back up her internal logic, Maou smiled and nodded. "I don't think you need to get all formal about it," he said. "Unless it's really busy or they're causing some kind of scene, you can talk for a bit in the corner somewhere and nobody's gonna care at all. That's all it'll probably be, won't it?"

"Yeah, I think so…um…"

Chiho found it strangely difficult to look Maou in the eye today. She only barely stammered out her reply, too.

Maou looked back and chuckled, as if recalling something.

"It's always kind of awkward when someone you know really well is watching you work, isn't it? But it'd be rude to just treat them like any other customer, too…"

Something about the display relieved Chiho. It was the same way with everyone else after all.

"Like, I never used to think about saying things like 'Good morning, sir' and 'Thank you' to my retainers back in the day. I feel kinda bad about it now."

If Maou had his own qualms about this social situation, then maybe Chiho had every right to eye it with dread. It made sense.

But something else sprang up in Chiho's mind. Maou had just used a word she was a little unfamiliar with. His "retainers"? What were those? Judging by the context, nothing to do with going to the dentist.

Maou, failing to notice this mild concern, looked toward Chiho and nodded. "Guess you just gotta read the situation and go with the flow, huh?"

"Um… Oh. Yeah, I guess you're right. Thank you! Sorry I'm asking such a pointless question."

The concern was really just a tiny ripple in her mind, quickly drowned out by the fact that Maou was looking right into her eyes. The awkward silence made her bow politely, and then it was gone entirely.

"Oh, it's fine, it's fine! I mean, when I first started working here, I even asked someone if it was okay to toss out the empty plastic bottles customers left behind. If anything, it's good that you're asking about that, Chi. It shows that you don't want to be caught messing around on the clock."

"H-hyeahh!"

"Huh?"

"Oh, um, yeah! Thank you very much!"

"Sure. Boy, you're a ball of energy today, Chi."

Chiho was having the worst problem keeping herself from stuttering around Maou lately. Being called "Chi" twice in rapid succession made her voice go into volume-overdrive mode, in a feeble attempt to cover up her embarrassment. It didn't work. All that hesitating last night, and now Maou was just spouting off "Chi, Chi" like a voice clip on repeat. She didn't mind it with the rest of the crew, but when Maou used that term, she just couldn't contain herself.

"Did they say when they'd be showing up?"

"Huh? Who?"

"Your friends."

"Oh… Um, umm, I don't know yet. I'm not even sure if they're showing at all or not…"

"Ah, all right. That'll make it even harder to relax, won't it? Like, I remember getting all nervous when a friend of mine said he'd come visit me in here, too. Try not to freak out too much, though, 'cause you'll wind up making careless errors that way."

Her friends had nothing to do with this current freakout. *That* was all about—

"Um, um, um, I'm gonna go do the 'Three PM Number Ten' check!"

"Oh? Sure thing. Thanks."

Unable to stand on the spot a moment longer, Chiho rather forcefully extracted herself from the conversation and escaped into the bathroom, Maou blessedly no longer in her field of vision.

"...Must be some tough friends to deal with," Maou mused as he watched her go.

"Number Ten" was crew slang for the bathroom, a term invented so they could discuss the toilets in public without spoiling customers' lunches. MgRonald stipulated hourly cleanliness checks, and that was what Chiho did now, writing her name on the inspection sheet taped to the wall next to the sinks.

"...Agh!"

Right above the three PM slot on the sheet was "MAOU," written in blocky, stereotypically mannish letting. He must have covered the two PM check.

"Uh, Maou, Chiho... Ahh! I messed it up! Wait, I...I didn't mean to...!"

She had written just her first name right in the middle of her slot. In a panic, she crossed it out and scribbled "Sasaki" into what little space remained on the side.

"This is getting *sooo* embarrassing."

She had no idea why she was obsessing over Maou so much. Whatever the cause, just thinking about him made it impossible to keep her cool. Having Kaori and Yoshiya show up when she was in a state like this would be even worse of a catastrophe.

Chiho left the bathroom, not particularly tired but her head still drooped down low.

"Oh, *there* you are, Sasaki!"

"Aaagh!"

Right in front of her was Yoshiya, practically bellowing out loud as he came up to Chiho in his street clothes.

"Ooh, Sasachi!" said Kaori, right behind him. "You weren't at the registers, so we were worried you were someplace where we couldn't see you."

"Ohhhh, okay, um... Great. So, uhhhh..."

Chiho was utterly unprepared for this. Ignoring all potential embarrassment, she turned her eyes toward Maou at the counter. Yoshiya's yelp of excitement had already caught his attention. He sized the three of them up, nodded, then signaled something with his eyes.

They hadn't known each other long enough to communicate non-verbally with much success. But Chiho, deciding to take a "what would Maou do" approach, pieced herself together as much as she could and gave her two friends a light bow.

"Welcome to MgRonald, guys!" she said. "Feel free to head to the counter once you're ready to order!"

"...Hohh?"

"Oooh, she's doing it!"

She dared another glance at Maou on the way back up. He just smiled back—no nods, no head shakes. That must've passed muster with him. She guided them to the register she and Maou were manning at the moment.

"Ah, welcome back, both of you."

"...Oh! Are you the guy from a few weeks ago?!"

Maou bowed at Kaori.

"Did you actually remember me?" she asked.

"Well, Ms. Sasaki mentioned you were her friends, so I figured that would've been the case. I'm sorry you had to deal with that ruined handout."

"Wait, what? Do you guys know each other?"

Yoshiya, unaware of the spilled-soda episode, gaped at the exchange between his friend and the MgRonald cashier.

"Oh!" Maou turned to Chiho. "I have an idea, Sasaki."

"Huh?"

"Since these are your friends and all, how 'bout I have you handle the entire order and tray setting?"

"Wha? By myself?!"

Chiho was fairly shocked at this. "Tray setting" involved how items were placed on the trays for customers—there was a whole slew of regulations related to that—but Chiho's cashier experience so far involved only taking orders and handling payments.

Outside of peak hours, it was the cashier's responsibility to bring out drinks and sides, assuming no one else on duty was free to handle that. A full-fledged cashier did far more than run the register—within a limited target time, they had to hand over drinks, fries, and occasionally salads and desserts to customers.

Chiho had been schooled on how to do all this…but would it really work? During the few moments she stewed over this, Maou left the register station and exchanged a few words with Kaori, off to the side. Kaori nodded and took something out of her wallet.

"So this is the receipt from last time, but he said we could exchange this for the same stuff as before."

"Huhh?!"

It was the service receipt Kisaki mentioned to Chiho back when she was just another customer. Kaori was just as much a victim of the soda-handout disaster as Chiho, so it made sense that Kisaki had stepped up to give her a freebie.

"Oh, hey, I got a coupon, too, actually."

"All right!"

Yoshiya probably didn't plan it in advance—he never did—but he took out his phone, pressed a few buttons, and showed Chiho a screen with a coupon on it.

"Hang in there," Maou said as he took a step back, watching over his charge.

Chiho closed her eyes, focused her concentration on the challenge before her, and took a deep breath. She was being tested. She had to respond in kind.

"…Now, would you like to have the same items that are printed on this receipt?"

"Sure, that works."

"Perfect. There won't be any charge for those, then."

Chiho typed in the dessert-and-soda set printed on Kaori's receipt and tapped the "special menu" key, followed by the receipt code to confirm that this was a complimentary reimbursement. Confirming the total cost was zero yen, she tapped "OK" on the touch screen.

Yoshiya, meanwhile, was ordering a combo with his coupon. "Hey," he asked, "can I use this coupon, but get some nuggets with it instead of fries?"

Chiho tapped the "e-Money" button and advised Yoshiya to put his phone against the reader in front of the register. He did so. The LED on the reader device lit up a reassuring shade of blue.

"...I apologize, sir," she said, "but since this is a limited-time coupon, I'm afraid that except for sizes, I'm not allowed to make any changes or substitutions."

"Oh, okay. I'll take fries, then. Oh, and a fountain drink."

"All right." She tapped "OK" again to lock in the order. "That'll be a total of six hundred fifty yen, please."

"Ah, shoot, this is all I got. Can you break this?"

Yoshiya handed a brown banknote to Chiho. She made sure to consciously read the numerical value on it as she accepted it.

"Certainly. Out of ten thousand yen... Change check, please!"

She called for another crewmember to first confirm the bill's value, then check to make sure the correct number of banknotes were provided as change.

"I'm sorry again, sir, but I'll have to provide your change in smaller bills. Is that all right?"

Since they were past the lunch rush, there were no more five-thousand-yen bills left in the register, forcing Chiho to give Yoshiya nine one-thousand-yen bills instead. She counted each one as she placed them in Yoshiya's hand.

"Eight...nine thousand...and three hundred fifty yen is your change. Is one tray all right?"

"Yeah, sure."

"Great. I'll have your order ready in just a moment, so if I could have you step to the right…"

The moment she completed the order, the register's touch screen shifted to a screen displaying her customers' wait time. Her job was to put the entire order on the tray and bring it over to them before the display turned red. It was April, and the heater was still on at low speed. The dessert would have to come out last to keep it from melting.

Chiho checked to make sure there were no customers behind her friends, then stuck her head into the kitchen area. She was just in time to witness the gratin-pie part of Yoshiya's Egg Gratin Burger getting flung into the fryer. Twenty seconds were all it took to fry it up. It then winged its way into a bun, where it was joined by a soft-boiled egg, some lettuce, and the mythical special sauce.

She figured she would begin constructing the tray with the fries, which were never as affected by room temperature as other items. She glanced over…

"!!"

…then changed tactics. Two sodas were filled and topped. She took the dessert out of the freezer, wiping the frost off the top. The gratin burger chose that exact time to trundle its way down the conveyor.

Chiho tapped the "Seat Wait" button on the wait-monitor screen, then placed the burger, drinks, dessert, and a plastic number panel on the tray.

"I apologize," she said as she handed it to Kaori. "We're working on a new batch of fries right now, so keep this number out and I'll be happy to bring a fresh set to your table."

"Ooh, nice. Good timing."

Yoshiya couldn't have been happier.

"All right. Enjoy your meal!"

"Yep."

"Thanks, Sasachi."

The two of them walked over to a table with surprisingly little complaint. Chiho found herself sneaking glances behind her shoulder through the whole process, but it didn't seem like anything she did gave them a bad impression.

As she watched them take a faraway seat by the window, Maou sidled back up to her.

"Chi?" he said.

"Um, yeah?"

More than anything, it was Maou's evaluation that mattered to her the most. She had learned nearly everything she knew about this job from him. She'd never forgive herself if she made any mistakes with him watching.

But that moment of anxiety disappeared once Maou gave her a smile and a nod.

"That was great," he said. "Like, I taught all that to you once, and you had it *down*. No mistakes at all."

"...Yes!"

A wave of joy that was hard to describe rushed over Chiho. She pumped her fist in the air.

"I thought you'd get stuck on typing in the receipt or handling the fry gap, but you handled all that like a pro. I'm not sure you even need me supervising you any longer."

"Um...really? I-I don't like that!"

Chiho blurted it out without thinking.

"Oh?"

"Um...huh? No, um, I mean, I think that'd still be kinda tough, is all. I don't think I'm *that* far advanced..."

"Well, no, I'm not gonna leave you all alone or anything. But if you're this quick of a learner, I bet Kisaki's gonna have us get into the real nitty-gritty stuff before too long... Oh, fries're done."

"Oops!"

An electronic beep indicated the new batch was ready to go, and the golden strands of deliciousness were lifted up from the oil in their metal basket.

"I'll show you how to salt the fries later on. I'll do it this time, since we've got customers waiting on 'em… Here we go."

Maou handed her the medium fries destined for Yoshiya's stomach.

"…!"

Their fingertips met for a moment, causing Chiho to inhale a little in surprise. Maou registered no particular response as he also provided a new tray and some napkins.

"You guys can chat a bit if you want," he said. "It's pretty slow right now."

"Oh, are—are you sure?"

"Sure. Have fun. Just don't make it too long."

"Cool! Thank you!" Chiho gave a quick bow and headed for Kaori and Yoshiya's table.

"Here you go!" she announced. "One fresh medium fries for you!"

"Ooh!"

Chiho placed the tray down, took the plastic number, and reverted from her all-business smile to her normal expression.

"So, um…that's pretty much how it is around here."

After all that, this was *still* a bit embarrassing for her.

"Oh, is it okay to talk?" Kaori glanced back at Maou behind the counter, gauging his response.

"Yeah, he said I could chat a little bit."

Kaori nodded approvingly. "Wow, that's pretty kind of him." Then she gave Chiho a good look, taking the time to study her from head to toe.

"I think that uniform looks good on you," she observed.

"Huh? Oh, uh, you think?"

"Definitely," Yoshiya agreed. "Like, totally grown-up."

"I am *not*!"

Chiho fanned herself with the number placard, her face starting to go flush.

"Yoshiya, would you stop staring at her legs, please?"

"I'm not doing anything like that, Shoji! Plus, that whole customer service thing you were doing? You looked like you had it down pat."

"Yeah," Kaori said. "I think you're a lot better at it than the girls at my last job, anyway."

"Really? Well, thanks."

Being looked at was embarrassing enough. This flurry of compliments was only making it worse.

"Seeing you like this… I dunno, maybe I really should get a job. Kaori keeps telling me this is a good location, too."

As always, it was hard to tell how serious Yoshiya was being. Kaori scowled at him.

"Here we go again…"

"What? I really mean it."

"Yeah?" Kaori sneered. "Even if you did, you still wouldn't be half as good at it as Sasachi. I mean, I know *I* couldn't last too long in here."

"Huh?"

Both Chiho and Yoshiya gave Kaori puzzled looks. She had said the exact opposite to Chiho earlier.

Then there was a shout from the counter. "Sasaki! You got a moment?" She must have idled for too long.

"Sorry, guys. Better get going."

"Sure thing."

"Have fun!"

Chiho left the table and jogged up to the counter.

"We have another customer who wanted to say hello, Sasaki."

"Oh?"

What, to me? Unsure what this was about, Chiho glanced at the customer next to her.

"Ah!"

Chiho held her breath for a moment. The large, well-built foreigner from before was standing there—the one who had made her spill her drink all over her handout and, in an indirect way, caused her to seek this job in the first place.

"Um, hello there!" Chiho began in Japanese. "Thanks for coming!"

Maou was kind enough to provide interpretation. "'I was surprised to see you got a job here,' he said. He wanted to know if that handout from before was okay."

"Yeah. I haven't filled it out yet, actually. But I think with this job, I'm starting to see what kind of stuff I wanna do after graduating."

"'I had a lot of trouble figuring out my future when I was in school, too. I kind of dodged the issue during school, unlike you, and it bit me in the rear later on, but I'm pretty proud of the career I have now.'"

"What kind of work do you do, sir?"

"Um, 'I'm an art dealer from Helsinki who sells Japanese paintbrushes. There's nothing else in the world that beats them in quality.' Wow, I didn't know that."

"Helsinki?" Chiho said. "Are you from Finland?"

The man eagerly nodded.

"He said he's going back to Helsinki tomorrow, but he was kind of worried over whether it worked out okay with you, so he thought he'd try coming back here."

"Well, thanks to him, I think I've found myself a pretty good job. I don't really know about my future yet, but I hope you'll come back here next time you're in Japan. I'll try to make sure I have some good news for you by then."

"'Absolutely,' he says. 'Good luck. And I promise you, the things you learn in school really do help you out in the future.'"

"Thanks!" Chiho gave a brisk nod of her own. "Oh, Maou?"

"Yeah?"

"...Could you tell him that I'll try my best to talk to him directly next time?"

✳

"..."

"You see that? No way you could handle that job with people like *that* around you. They'd crush you for being so useless. And if you really wanna drop out of school, I ain't gonna stop you, but I don't think you're cut out to work here right now."

"..."

"Yoshiya?"

"Hey, um, Shoji?"

"Hmm?"

"...Where's Finland?"

"Yoshiyaaaa... I'll forgive you for not knowing Helsinki, but come on! Finland's in northern Europe! It's in the EU and everything! You didn't even know that and you think you can work with Sasachi? Geez."

"And people go all the way from there to buy brushes from us?"

"I guess so, unless that guy messed up the translation. I doubt it, though."

"What do they use them for?"

"How would I know? If you care that much, ask him."

"How?"

"Ask that Maou dude, or try your a-*maaaazing* English skills on him."

"..."

❋

Six in the evening. Chiho's friends stuck around long enough to meet up with her at the end of her shift. Luckily for them, it never got crowded enough that the crew felt obliged to boot them from their table.

Thanks to the combined efforts of Maou, Kaori, and Yoshiya, Chiho was now confident enough to work through an entire order herself. The learning process was still only beginning for her, but she still found the shift remarkably fulfilling.

"Hey, Sasaki?" Yoshiya quietly asked on the way back.

"Hmm? What is it?"

"Who's that guy on your team who knows English? Is he in college, or did he live in the U.S. or something?"

"I don't think so. I tried asking him once, but he said he learned English because he thought it'd help him with work. We get a lot of international visitors from the offices near the station, actually."

"He got *that* good at it just for a fast-food job?"

Chiho had the same question. It wasn't a bad talent to have, of course, but it did seem like overkill.

"Say," she replied, "do you know what language they speak in Finland?"

"Huh? Not English?"

Chiho shook her head. "I guess they have their own language. It's called Finnish, and it's very different from English. But after that guy graduated from school, he learned how to speak English and German pretty much just studying by himself. He got it all from schoolbooks."

"…He's gotta be pretty smart, then."

"He didn't go to college, Yoshiya."

Yoshiya fell silent. Chiho sneaked a glance at him as she recalled Kisaki's advice. Deciding on your future was nothing more than deciding what to do tomorrow, then doing it over and over again. Maou and their Finnish-speaking visitor learned English in their own respective "todays" because they figured they'd need it "tomorrow." And maybe they didn't know what they'd be doing a year from now, but they knew that neither tomorrow nor 365 tomorrows from now would be the exact same as today. To prepare for that, the more weapons you had, the better.

And even if that globe-trotting art dealer didn't come back to Japan tomorrow, he might come back next month. Chiho at least owed him an English greeting or two, she reasoned. Whether that would pay dividends for her a year or two years from now was another issue, but…still.

"What I'm saying, Yoshiya, is that you can't do anything for other people if you can't even make an effort for yourself."

That didn't just apply to Maou. It applied to Kisaki, her other supervisors, and everyone else on the crew. They could all make a daily effort, because they wanted to work for the sake of others.

Yoshiya turned back at Chiho. "…What do you mean?" he asked.

She laughed and smiled a devilish grin.

"Not telling!"

After all the effort she needed to figure it out, she wasn't about to let Yoshiya in on the secret that easily.

"You know," she added, "I think I could fill out that survey for real now."

"Whoa, you haven't done it yet?" Kaori exclaimed.

"Well, for now, I put down that I want to go to a college with a good *kyudo* program. That's not a total lie, and that's about the best thing I could think of anyway. If they don't like it at the conference, I'll think about it then."

"...What're you two girls talking about?"

From that point until they all went their separate ways, Yoshiya's face looked like he was having stomach cramps.

※

The day of conferences had arrived.

Yoshiya's session was scheduled first, followed by Chiho's and Kaori's. All of them, along with their parents, were seated on chairs lined up in the hallway. And after all that griping on Yoshiya's part, there was his mother, seated right there next to him. Judging how he talked about his brothers, Chiho was expecting an ultrastrict taskmaster. Instead she was small, slightly plump, and supremely mild-mannered.

Ever since his visit to Chiho's workplace, Yoshiya had grown oddly quiet. It seemed to irk Kaori a little, since fewer things said meant fewer chances to wheedle him.

"Mrs. Kohmura?" said Mr. Ando, inviting mother and son into the classroom. The woman nodded at Chiho and Kaori as she passed by, but Yoshiya didn't bother to so much as glance at them.

"Sasachi, Sasachi!"

Kaori gestured at Chiho the moment the door closed, inviting her to come over as she crouched down by the slit below the classroom entrance.

"K-Kao, we can't..."

"Um, Kaori?"

Chiho and Kaori's mother simultaneously admonished her for so brazenly trying to listen in. But she shouldn't have bothered anyway.

"...Well, Mrs. Kohmura, thanks very much for taking the time out to attend this conference today."

Mr. Ando's booming voice was clearly audible through the door. All three of them rolled their eyes. Sasahata North was in a fairly old school building, so no matter how tightly the doors were fastened, there was practically no soundproofing provided at all.

"...I'll be in the bathroom," Chiho's mother chuckled as she stood up. "Ooh, maybe I should while I have the chance, too," Kaori's mother added. As adults, they both must've felt uncomfortable listening in.

Once they disappeared down the hall, Chiho and Kaori looked at each other.

"...Uh, me too," Chiho said, figuring she should join the throng.

"No," whispered Kaori, pushing her back down. "We have to wait here. Besides, Yoshiya's been acting weird lately. I'm startin' to wonder if he had some kinda revelation in his mind or something."

"Oh, Kaori, how do you even know we can hear him in—"

"So, Kohmura, I apologize that there's no easy way to say this, but with your current grades, getting into a university English-literature program's gonna be pretty tough. Where'd *that* desire come from, all of a sudden?"

"..."

Mr. Ando had nothing if not an inadvertently perfect sense of comic timing. Chiho was about ready to crack up, as was Kaori. *Yoshiya*, studying *English literature*?!

"...Mr. Ando," Yoshiya replied in a reserved voice before the girls could regain their composure, "I'm pretty sure you know this already, but my brothers are pretty much geniuses. But... I know my grades aren't any good, but I could just never get myself to wanna follow in their footsteps. I'm sure they both had really clear reasons why they wanted to be judges or doctors or whatever, but someone like me... I don't really have the will to try going down this well-trodden path to success like everyone else does. I just don't think it would work."

"No? I don't think that's necessarily a bad approach, but...what, then?"

Yoshiya let out a deep, deliberate sigh.

"............Finland."

Chiho and Kaori exchanged amused glances again.

"Huh?"

"Mr. Ando, what do you think it's like to be a person from Finland who goes to Japan so he can purchase paintbrushes to sell back home?"

"Um, pardon me?"

"Do you think he could make a living from that?"

"I'm...not exactly sure where this is going."

Chiho couldn't blame Mr. Ando for his confusion.

"I was just thinking," Yoshiya continued. "You say that being a doctor or working for the government's really stable work that makes a lot of money, but it's not like they just hand you a check the moment you get one of those jobs. You have to really *work* for the government before you get paid, you know? Like, you get paid for teaching classes to us, right? It's not just a matter of landing a stable job—you're a teacher, Mr. Ando, because this job gives you something to dream about or work for, right?"

"Mmm, well, yeah, certainly."

"Some of my friends have been working part-time lately, and I just figured...like, maybe I shouldn't be trying to just pursue some job title or other. I should try to figure out what I should do if I wanna be able to pursue whatever job I think's worth striving for in the future. So..."

Yoshiya paused for a moment, perhaps searching for the right words.

"...This guy I saw, I don't think he studied in school just so he could go to Japan and be a paintbrush dealer. But let's say that, for some reason or another, that's what I wind up doing in the future. I started thinking about what I'd need to do now for that, and…I know I just failed it in the mock exam, but I think English is a big part of it. But I'm not smart or anything, and I know I'll get all lazy if I don't have a real goal to strive for, so I thought I'd aim for some kind of high-level English-literature program. That kind of thing."

"…"

Before they knew it, Chiho and Kaori were hanging on Yoshiya's every word, faces focused on the door.

"…And what do you think of that, Mrs. Kohmura?" a still-confused Mr. Ando asked.

"…I think that myself, my husband, and Yoshiya's brothers have taken exactly the kind of well-trodden path he was talking about. My husband has a job in government administration, and before we got married, I was a teacher myself."

"Ah!"

That surprised Chiho. She instantly began to wish Yoshiya hadn't been so secretive about his family. She peeked at Kaori. Judging by the way she was holding her breath and staring daggers at the door, she must not have known, either.

"It wasn't our intention to force the same path on Yoshiya, but I do think being surrounded by people like ourselves made things… uncomfortable for him. I'm worried that he thought we forced his brothers down the paths they took, too."

"…Aw, nothing like *that*, Mom."

"Basically, if our children had a goal in life, I didn't think it was our place to tell them what to do or not do. Once that decision is made, that's going to result in something real, whether it's good or bad. So I know he can be a handful sometimes, Mr. Ando, but I hope you'll be willing to give him the guidance he'll need for that goal… I don't know how Finland got into his mind, but the next time we go on vacation, I'll make sure he comes along to interpret for us."

That last sentence was probably intended for her son. There was nothing chiding in it. It was the voice of a mother who always cared for her children—just like how Riho, Chiho's mother, cared for hers.

"Yeah," Yoshiya said. "Well, I'm still failing it right now, so don't get your hopes up too high."

"Well, you're going to work on that, aren't you?"

The conversation—a sort of mix of conference and idle chitchat—continued for a while longer before they heard the clatter of chairs against the floor. Chiho and Kaori sat straight back on their chairs, as if nothing was amiss.

"*Yoshiya*, of all people," Kaori whispered just before the Kohmuras left the room with Mr. Ando. It didn't escape Chiho's ears.

"Thanks again, Mrs. Kohmura. Now, Sasaki... Hmm? Where did your mother go?"

"Oh, she's in the bathroom. She should be back in a sec..."

"Sorry, sorry!" exclaimed Riho, trotting down the hallway on cue in her high heels.

"No problem. Right in here, please."

The Sasakis passed by the Kohmuras as they went in. As they did, Chiho dared a question to Yoshiya.

"Do you still wanna work?"

Yoshiya didn't seem to understand why Chiho asked that. He frowned and turned his back to her.

"You guys won't stop bitching at me to study," he sheepishly said on the way out, "so I think I'll stick to that for now."

Kaori, expressionless, watched him leave.

Although Chiho didn't want to pat herself on the back too much, there was no doubt in her mind. Yoshiya had changed, and it wasn't entirely his doing, either. It was also thanks to Maou, and that Finnish art dealer, and probably what he saw of her at work, too.

The only regret she had was that Yoshiya's survey submission overlapped with hers. She had also listed English literature as one of her candidates, for most of the same reasons. That was what she wanted to build on, and right now, that was one of the things she knew she *could* build on.

The world was a big place—far bigger than what students like herself could see, or even try to see. There was no guarantee that the world in front of her eyes right now would be the same as the one she saw next year. And if that was the case, she reasoned that her job was something to start with, so that she could grasp and earn the things she needed to plunge into that new world. That, she thought, was the path she had to take.

Career guidance, after all, wasn't a final goal. It was just another checkpoint along the way.

Now Chiho very much *was* patting herself on the back. She realized it even as she was trying to figure out a way to explain the reasoning for her choice without duplicating Yoshiya's approach too much. Even she had to admit it was awfully small-minded of her.

"Well," Mr. Ando began, "with your grades, Sasaki, I think you could be looking at a pretty decent choice of universities, liberal arts or not. You listed your first aspiration as English literature; could you explain to me why?"

It wasn't like she needed a single reason for it, one almighty motive for putting in the effort. She wasn't Yoshiya, but the motive driving her forward was just as easy to follow as his. It was in that *kai* pose the *kyudo* club leader put on for her when she first joined this school. It lay in the work being done by all the grown-ups around her. And it was all linked together by that piece of paper in Mr. Ando's hands right now.

She wanted to be there. She wanted to see that same world.

"I…I have people in my life that I respect. People whose paths I want to follow."

She wanted to be on an even keel with them. With him. To experience the same world as him.

✳

This was my story. From back when I was just a clueless high-school teen. The story of Chiho Sasaki, a girl prepared for a different tomorrow in her life—although maybe not one that would change the entire world at the end of it.

Not even two weeks after that parent-teacher conference, I found out the truth. And once I did, my world unfolded in ways that it never had for me before. I was an everyday teen thrust into a life-or-death struggle, with the future of entire nations and countless lives in the balance.

But just a few days before, it had all been different...

THE AUTHOR, THE AFTERWORD, AND YOU!

Caution: This afterword contains a few spoilers. If you're the type of person who likes to flip to the back and check out the afterword first, consider yourself warned.

It should be noted that I, Satoshi Wagahara, have never actually worked any of the jobs, part-time or not, that have been featured in Volumes 1 through 6 of *The Devil Is a Part-Timer!* The Devil might have, but I haven't. Or didn't. Because Volume 7 is actually different—the four stories in this volume all owe their genesis to my own past experiences.

In each of these tales, I've introduced a new element—to be specific, a new character or two—to the usual gang that populates this series, from the Devil King and Hero on down. My hope is that each one brings a new element to this saga of everyday life and helps make it not so everyday after all.

The Devil Pledges to Stay Legitimate:
This story begins, oh, I'd say around thirty seconds after the end of Volume 2. The theme should be pretty obvious: If a challenge comes along, stay calm and talk it over with someone first.

Scams like these have been fodder for hidden camera–type news shows for a while now. It seems like such a stupid trick, but damn if it doesn't work often enough to be profitable.

In my case, I was out in business attire one morning when a guy running a stand near my local rail station attempted to sell me a set of four Claude Blanchet pears. That was the inspiration for this story. I wasn't going to an office job or anything, but I wonder what made the guy think a businessman would be hankering for an armful of semiripe fruit during the morning rush...

The Devil Plucks a Cat Off the Street:

Just before my first novel made its debut, the parakeet I shared the previous sixteen years of my life with at my family home passed away from old age. It was something of a miracle it had toughed it out for that long (I'd say it was around 130 in people years), and between the cataracts and the two different strokes it'd had over the years, it was a fighter to the core.

During that whole ordeal, though, we were lucky enough to work with an extremely kind veterinarian. It ultimately led to this story—one that I hope helps express my appreciation for him and my wish that all pets enjoy happy lives.

By the way, the front yard of this house was also the location of not one, but four semi-abandoned kitten litters—four years in a row, all from the same mother. She was too cute to attempt to banish from the place for good, but every time she used my father's shiitake-mushroom growing trees as scratching posts, his stance on the subject became sorely, *sorely* tested.

The Devil and the Hero Go Futon Shopping:

It was a real shock to me how much my cousin's daughter (one of the inspirations for Alas Ramus) grew over the course of a single year. It was the same deal when I searched for a birthday present for one of my friend's babies. All the advice the person at the store gave me was bewildering. I have no idea how anyone can keep up with how fast they grow—and all the stuff they have to buy along the way! The scale is staggering.

If Maou and Emi keep on dragging their feet like this, the passage of time's only gonna make things worse for them. Get moving, people!

A Few Days Before: The Teenager Is a Part-Timer!:
A prequel that tells the story of Chiho Sasaki and Sadao Maou, leading right up to the first *Devil* novel. This tale was originally written for that very book.

I know Chiho's starting to acquire some fairly superhuman traits over in the main plotline, but back around this time, she really was just an ordinary teen—as ordinary as teens ever really get, that is. Normally, she tends to act as polite as possible around the other characters, since she's always the youngest out of all of them. When I started writing this, mainly I just wanted to depict her acting a lot more informal with her peers at school. Then the story took on a life of its own, you could say.

They say there's an old proverb from China or somewhere that says, "May you live in interesting times." *Interesting*, of course, can mean so many things in so many situations. In my case, the amount of mental gymnastics I've engaged in to help me blow through deadlines without any regrets certainly qualifies as "interesting," I think, even though my editor has wanted to club me for it multiple times. Next time, I'll try to be a little quicker with working casual high school conversations into an actual story.

Anyway, this volume will be in readers' hands no sooner than February 10, 2013. Two months after that, in April, the *Devil Is a Part-Timer!* anime will make its television debut. Volume 8 of the *Devil* novel series will hit stores on April 10 as well, just in time for my third year of devoting myself to this tale. This world keeps on growing and growing, and I hope you'll enjoy the journey that lies ahead for it.

No matter how far it expands, though, this is still just the story of a bunch of people enjoying three square meals a day, cherishing every moment of their lives as they find out where life takes them next. I'd love a chance to write more easygoing portraits of daily life like what this volume offers, but—just like them—I'll have to see what the future brings.

Until next time!

CONGRATULATIONS ON RELEASING VOLUME 7! THIS IS AKIO HIIRAGI, ARTIST FOR THE COMIC VERSION RUNNING IN DENGEKI DAIOH MAGAZINE. RIGHT NOW (FEBRUARY 2013), I'M TACKLING THE PART OF THE STORY WHERE SUZUNO MAKES HER DEBUT. IT'S A LOT OF FUN, ESPECIALLY SINCE IT'S ABOUT TIME VILLA ROSA SASAZUKA HAD A LITTLE REFINEMENT ADDED TO IT!

SUZUNO IN THE SPRING

AKIO HIIRAGI

SPECIAL GUEST 01

SPECIAL GUEST **02**

VOLUME 7'S OUT!
CONGRATULATIONS!

MY NAME'S KURONE MISHIMA, AND I WRITE
THE DEVIL IS A PART-TIMER! HIGH SCHOOL!,
A SPIN-OFF COMIC VERSION OF THE ORIGINAL
NOVELS! I LOVE DRAWING THE EMILIA/ALAS
RAMUS COMBO TOGETHER... THEY'RE SO CUTE! ♪

MAKE SURE TO
CHECK OUT HIGH SCHOOL!
VOLUME 1, OUT NOW!

KURONE MISHIMA

THE DEVIL IS A PART-TIMER! 7
SPECIAL END-OF-BOOK BONUS

RÉSUMÉ
COLLECTION

NAME
Mayumi Kisaki

DATE OF BIRTH	AGE	GENDER
September 25, 198X	26	F

ADDRESS
Nishihara Apartments #203
X-X-X Nishihara, Shibuya-ku, Tokyo

TELEPHONE NUMBER
030-0000-0000

PAST EXPERIENCE	
199X:	Graduated from Sasahata Central High School, Tokyo
200X:	Entered Meiji University, College of Business Administration
200X:	Graduated from Meiji University, College of Business Administration
200X:	Joined MgRonald Japan Co., Ltd. (current position)

QUALIFICATIONS/CERTIFICATIONS
Food hygiene supervisor, fire protection manager, retail sales manager (level 2),
color coordinator (level 2), MgRonald Barista, TOEIC score: 860

SKILLS/HOBBIES
Work, cultivating talent, cooking, travel

REASON FOR APPLICATION
To make my dreams come true

PERSONAL GOALS
To stay on the front lines my whole life and never retire

COMMUTE TIME	FAMILY/DEPENDENTS	NAME OF GUARDIAN
Approx. 15 minutes walking	None	None
I'd like to live in the store if possible		

BASIC IDEA LINK TRAINING

1

TOP REQUIREMENT: BELIEVE, HEART AND SOUL, THAT YOU CAN COMMUNICATE YOUR WILL WITHOUT USING ANY SPEECH!

It's just like riding a bike without training wheels for the first time. The toughest part is really trusting in your body and mind and believing that you can do it, right? And once you manage that trick, it really is like riding a bike.

2

RELEASE THE "WILL" YOU WANT TO BRING ACROSS IN "ENERGY" FORM, AND YOU'RE WELL ON YOUR WAY.

Humans would use holy energy; demons would use, well, demonic energy. But that by itself isn't enough to get the message across to others. It's sort of like shouting in the middle of a huge crowd of people.

3

FOCUS ON WHO YOU WANT TO "RECEIVE" YOUR WILL.

You need a phone number to contact someone on their cell, and that's actually a perfect metaphor for picturing your Idea Link receiver in your mind. That's what Sariel says, at least, and I'm not sure I totally trust him on that, but...

4

MASTER ONE-ON-ONE CONVERSATION, AND YOU'RE OVER THE HUMP!

Such abilities can be applied in many ways—broadcasting, group calls with multiple people, long-range links, "tethering" between nonenergy users. For now, though, this is the extent of Chiho's already-commendable abilities. If she wishes to go further in depth, I would recommend an Ente Isla–based study program.